P9-DGV-991

LOCKDOWN

ALSO BY
WALTER DEAN MYERS

FICTION

AUTOBIOGRAPHY OF MY DEAD BROTHER
National Book Award Finalist

CRYSTAL

DOPE SICK

THE DREAM BEARER

GAME

HANDBOOK FOR BOYS: A NOVEL

IT AIN'T ALL FOR NOTHIN'

MONSTER
Michael L. Printz Award
Coretta Scott King Author Honor Book
National Book Award Finalist

THE MOUSE RAP

PATROL: AN AMERICAN SOLDIER IN VIETNAM
Jane Addams Children's Book Award

THE RIGHTEOUS REVENGE OF ARTEMIS BONNER

SCORPIONS
Newbery Honor Book

SHOOTER

THE STORY OF THE THREE KINGDOMS

STREET LOVE

NONFICTION

ANGEL TO ANGEL:
A MOTHER'S GIFT OF LOVE

BAD BOY: A MEMOIR

BROWN ANGELS:
AN ALBUM OF PICTURES AND VERSE

THE HARLEM HELLFIGHTERS:
WHEN PRIDE MET COURAGE

IDA B. WELLS: LET THE TRUTH BE TOLD

I'VE SEEN THE PROMISED LAND:
THE LIFE OF DR. MARTIN LUTHER KING, JR.

MALCOLM X: A FIRE BURNING BRIGHTLY

MUHAMMAD ALI: THE PEOPLE'S CHAMPION

NOW IS YOUR TIME!:
THE AFRICAN-AMERICAN STRUGGLE FOR FREEDOM
Coretta Scott King Author Award

WALTER DEAN MYERS

LOCKDOWN

Amistad is an imprint of HarperCollins Publishers.

Lockdown

Library of Congress Cataloging-in-Publication Data
Myers, Walter Dean, date
Lockdown / Walter Dean Myers. — 1st ed.
p. cm.
Summary: Teenage Reese, serving time at a juvenile detention facility, gets a lesson in making it through hard times from an unlikely friend with a harrowing past.
ISBN 978-0-06-121480-6 (trade bdg.)
ISBN 978-0-06-121481-3 (lib. bdg.)
[1. Juvenile delinquents—Fiction. 2. Juvenile detention homes—Fiction. 3. Conduct of life—Fiction. 4. Friendship—Fiction. 5. Self-perception—Fiction. 6. Old age—Fiction. 7. African Americans—Fiction.] I. Title.
PZ7.M992Lo 2010 2009007287
[Fic]—dc22 CIP
AC

Typography by Andrea Vandergrift
11 12 13 14 LP/RRDH 10 9 8 7 6
❖
First Edition

To Phoebe Yeh, editor and friend

CHAPTER 1

"I hope you mess this up! I hope you blow it big-time! You're supposed to be smart. You think you're smart, right?"

"Sir . . ."

"Shut up, worm!" Mr. Pugh looked over his shoulder at me. "If you had any smarts, you'd be out on the streets. But you're in jail, ain't you? Ain't you?"

"Yes, sir."

"And you know this work program is bullshit. Just more work for me and the staff. But I'm counting on you, worm. All you got to do is walk away when nobody's looking. When they catch you, I'm going to put you in a hole so deep, you won't even remember what daylight looks like."

The van stopped. I could see Mr. Pugh looking out the window. Then he got out and came around the back. I was handcuffed to the rail, and he climbed in and unhooked me.

"Turn around."

I hated having my hands cuffed behind me—all the kids did—but I twisted around in the van like he said. He cuffed me, then pulled me out of the van by my sleeve. I stumbled a little but I didn't fall. I stood behind the van with my head down like I was supposed to as he locked it up. Then he took me by the arm and led me to a side door.

He stopped just inside the door while he looked around; then he took me over to a woman sitting behind a desk. She was small, Spanishy looking, with dark eyes that went quickly from me to Mr. Pugh.

"Yes?"

"I'm here to see a Father Santora," Mr. Pugh said. "This is the inmate."

The receptionist smiled at me, then picked up the phone on her desk and made a call.

"The people from Progress are here, Father," she said into the phone.

Mr. Pugh was a big man, as wide as he was tall,

but the thing that got to you was that he didn't have any eyebrows. His skin was really white and he was bald, so it looked like his face ran all the way up his head. I knew he didn't want to have to drive me to the nursing home, but I didn't care.

Mr. Pugh didn't uncuff me until the man from the hospital had signed the papers.

"I'll be back to pick him up at four," Mr. Pugh said. "I'll leave a pair of cuffs in case you need them."

I watched as Mr. Pugh headed for the door. I used to think I couldn't hate anyone as much as I hated my father, but Mr. Pugh was coming close.

"Well, welcome to Evergreen," the man said. "I'm Father Santora and I run the facility. This is Sonya, and your name is . . ." He looked at the paper. "Maurice Anderson. Do you mind if we call you Maurice?"

"Most people I know call me Reese," I said.

"Okay, then we'll call you Reese," Father Santora said. "You'll be coming here ten days a month for the next eight weeks in your work-release program. We think you'll like it here."

He left the handcuffs with Sonya and took me into the elevator. He looked okay, but a lot of people looked okay.

"Evergreen is basically a facility for senior citizens," Father Santora said. "It's not a hospital so much as a refuge. People reach a stage in their lives where they need to have assistance from day to day."

"What am I going to be doing here?" I asked.

"You'll be working under Mrs. Silvey," he said. "She sees to the comfort of the residents. It'll probably be cleaning the hallways or running errands for the seniors. But she'll let you know. How old are you?"

"Fourteen. I'll be fifteen next month."

"You play basketball?" he asked, smiling.

"No, not really," I said.

Father Santora asked me if I minded sitting down on a bench in one of the hallways and said he was going to look for Mrs. Silvey. I said it was fine with me.

The place smelled like a hospital. I saw two old guys walking down toward the end of the hall holding hands. They were really old looking and one of them was stooped over, so I figured he was sick.

I sat there for a while and then Father Santora came back with a woman. I stood up and kind of nodded.

She looked me up and down and asked me how tall I was.

"I don't know," I said. "Maybe about five five."

"You're five seven," she said. "Maybe five six and a half. You have family in the city?"

"Yes, ma'am."

"Well, welcome to Evergreen. Come with me."

Father Santora was smiling as I left with the lady. She took me down the hallway and up a flight of stairs to the next floor. It was like a big dayroom, and people were sitting around playing cards or watching television. She took me to a closet and opened it. Inside there was a small plastic bucket and a kind of stick with a grabber on it to pick up paper off the ground.

"There's a lot of paper and trash on the floor," she said. "Sometimes the residents get careless. I want you to go around and pick up anything you recognize as trash. If someone argues with you, says that something isn't trash, then you either put it back where you found it or offer it to them. You understand that?"

"Yes, ma'am."

"And I don't want you touching anything nasty with your hands," she said. "And I need you to wash your hands at least twice a day and keep your hands out of your face and especially away from your eyes. I don't want you getting sick.

"Never argue with anyone here," she went on. "Do you understand that?"

"Yes, ma'am."

"Father Santora said they call you Reese, is that right?"

"Yes, ma'am."

"Okay, Reese. So, you'll be working here from ten to four. At twelve, after the residents have eaten, you'll eat with the staff. It's a very informal, catch-as-catch-can kind of meal. At three thirty you'll clean up and get ready to go back to Progress. How long have you been there?"

"Twenty-two months."

She looked at me like she was surprised, but she didn't say anything.

"My office is on this floor. It's room 307. If you can't remember that, Simi or Nancy—they're on our staff and will work directly with you—will tell you. If you have a problem you'll come to me, right?"

"Yes, ma'am."

"And Reese." She stopped and took a deep breath. "Many of the residents here are on medication.

You're not to touch any of the medications for any reason. Even if you see a bottle on the floor, you'll tell Simi or Nancy. Do you understand that?"

"Yeah."

She left me, and I took the bucket and grabber out of the closet. I noticed there were some hooks in the closet so I could hang my clothes if it was raining. I hoped it didn't rain on the days I was coming to Evergreen, because I didn't want them seeing me in my orange rain hood.

I walked around the dayroom most of the morning picking up little pieces of paper. Most of the people sitting around were white and they were all real old. I heard some of them talking and it wasn't in English, so I thought they might have been talking about me. I didn't care. It was better than being at the Progress Center.

A tiny little woman saw me coming near her and she took an orange off the tray she was sitting near and put it behind her back. I wanted to smile but I didn't. One man looked big and he had something wrong with the skin on his face. I thought maybe he was in some pain or something.

"Hey, what's your name?" another woman asked me.

I was about to tell her but she looked away.

I started walking away, but then she yelled at me and asked me my name again.

"Reese," I said.

"What kind of name is that?"

"And he's only got one name," another woman said. "Maybe his family couldn't afford two names."

"It's really Maurice," I said. "Maurice Anderson."

The day went by fast. I kept the floor clear, which was easy. I met two more people from the Evergreen staff at lunchtime. One was a short, heavy black girl with an African-sounding name. She talked on her cell phone all the while we were in the staff room, which was a little room on the second floor with a coffeepot, a microwave, and a small refrigerator.

The other one was a Puerto Rican guy. He said he did the maintenance work, but he looked like he couldn't see too good out of his thick glasses. There were sandwiches and soup for lunch. It was good. Or at least better than what we had at Progress.

Three thirty and I put the bucket and pickup thing back in the closet and washed up. Mrs. Silvey told me to wait on the first floor for the van. When I got there, a delivery guy was bringing packages and kidding around with the receptionist. I thought I would like to do that, have a regular job and kid around with people I met.

Mr. Pugh showed up at five minutes to four and made a motion for me to turn around. Sucker didn't have to do that and he knew it.

I turned around and he handcuffed me with the receptionist looking. That made me feel bad, but I knew he wanted me to feel bad.

He didn't say nothing on the way back to Progress, but I knew what he was waiting for. He took me into the reception room right away and closed the door.

"You know the routine," he said.

I stripped down and bent over while he searched me.

It was almost not worth it. I hated being searched, having Pugh or anybody putting their hands all up in me. But I knew if I got through the two months working at Evergreen and didn't mess up, I had a chance for an early out when my hearing came up. That's all I thought about as Pugh messed with me. Getting back out on the street again.

When I got back from Evergreen Mr. Cintron asked me how I liked it and I said I thought it was okay.

"Just okay?" he asked.

"They treated me okay," I said. "I wasn't locked in my room or nothing, so I guess it was okay."

"Well, that's your choice, Reese," he said. "You can spend the rest of your life in some kind of institution like this or you can be out there in the world. And what you got to keep in your head—what you got to focus on—is that 'okay' is a lot better than being in a place like this."

That was all good and everything, and I knew he was right, but I didn't know what was going down with me. Mr. Cintron talked about it like it was something easy. You go this way or you go that way.

Maybe for him it was easy.

He was cool, though. He was tall, about thirty-something or maybe even forty. He looked Spanish but he sounded pure white. He was the only one at Progress who I believed most of the time.

There were only twelve of us in Section A, and in the morning Mr. Pugh marched us to breakfast. When Mr. Wilson marched us to breakfast we could have our hands down by our sides, but when Mr. Pugh took us anywhere we had to have our hands behind our backs with our wrists crossed like we were handcuffed, even though we weren't. The breakfast was the same old stuff. Scrambled eggs, oatmeal, juice, and bologna. It was okay. I liked it when the bologna was burned sometimes. When I was home and Icy made breakfast, she burned everything. She liked to see the food cooking. It was burned but I didn't mind.

The word was that something was going to happen after dinner. When we finished breakfast and took the trays to the window for the dishwashers, I asked Play what was happening.

"Diego wants to jump Toon into the 3-5-7s," Play said.

"Toon?" I asked. "He ain't nothing but twelve!"

"And what's he going to do in the 3-5-7s?" Play said.

"Shut up!" Mr. Pugh hollered from across the room.

We lined up and went back to our quarters. I checked everything real quick because I didn't want any trouble. The floor was swept, the bed made, and the sink clean. I knew that as long as everything went down correct, I would stay on level one and in the early-release program. If I started getting demerits and fell into level three or four, then I wouldn't have any privileges and would have a harder time getting out early.

Eight o'clock and we went to school. Me, Leon, Diego, and this white girl named Kat were in the same class. They said she'd cut up a guy who was trying to mess with her and drank a soda while the guy was lying on the floor bleeding.

Play was fifteen and a nice guy, but he was facing juvy life for shooting a guy. His lawyer was still working on his case. Diego was fifteen and was doing a year for breaking and entering. Leon was fourteen and was in for shoplifting and punching a security guard. Toon was in because he wouldn't go to school or listen to nobody. He said his parents had been accountants in Mumbai before they came to the States. His real name was Deepak but he didn't look like a regular kid—he had this round face and big glasses like a cartoon character, so we all called him Toon. He liked that.

But jumping him into the 3-5-7 was just stupid. The 3-5-7 was a prison gang, and I couldn't see Toon being in no gang. I knew if they tried to jump him in, he would just fall and get beat up.

We did school, which was bull because we weren't learning anything. Play was too messed around with his case to even think about what was going on in the Revolutionary War, and nobody else really cared. I listened because I just wanted to do better than the others. That's how bad I wanted to be out in the world.

Mr. Wilson had us for lunch, and we knew we could talk if we weren't too loud. I asked Diego why he wanted to jump Toon into the 3-5-7.

"Why you want to know?" Diego came back.

"I just asked you a question, fool," I said.

"If I kick your ass will I still be a fool?" Diego looked at me across the table. "Don't be calling me no fool."

"If I stab you about forty-five times can I call you

a fool?" I asked him.

He sucked his teeth and looked away.

"I think he wants to jump in Toon because Toon's the only one in our section he can beat," Play said.

We all cracked on that but I thought it was true. Diego kept on talking about being in the 3-5-7 crew but I didn't believe him. They didn't do the light stuff he was always talking about. He was about my height but he had a mustache that made him look older. I knew what was going down with him, though. Mr. Pugh said that a guy from the 3-5-7 was scheduled to come to Progress Center. Diego knew the kid, and the way he was talking about him, it was like he was scared of him or something. So I figured he was going to try to punk somebody out to make his reputation.

I hoped he didn't mess with Toon, because I liked the little guy. I couldn't stand up for him and risk getting disciplined, though.

I can do some business with my hands if I got to. Willis, my brother, used to do some boxing and we used to spar around in the gym. Then he got shot and didn't have any more interest in fighting. I didn't like to fight in a ring or anything like that. It just didn't appeal to me, but when my father started hitting me all the time, I was glad I knew a little something. At least how to cover up so you won't get your face all messed up. Luther, that's my father's name, is the kind of dude who gets to drinking and telling himself he's doing you a favor by beating you up. That's why I hate him so much. You ain't supposed to be beating up your kids. Even if you are half drunk.

After lunch we had school from 12:15 to 2:15, which was more of the same. Some of the kids are smart, but they be having other things on their mind. Toon acted like he wanted to go to school. I don't know why he didn't want to go to school when he was out in the world, but I know this: He had a reason.

We had group 2:30 to 4:30, and they brought in a black guy who told us we could be something special if we tried. Same old, same old. He said he used to be a drug dealer. Play asked him what kind of watch he was wearing, and as soon as he had to look down at it, we knew he didn't have anything going on.

After group we went back to our section, and the guy who was supposed to be in the 3-5-7 was there. Diego called him Cobo. He was wearing a gray jumpsuit instead of an orange one, which meant he wasn't going to be at Progress very long. You could see Diego sucking up to the new guy and the new guy strutting around like he was bad.

"You got five days, maybe four, to be here before you go upstate to Replacement Center," Pugh said to Cobo. "You'd better behave yourself every minute of every day. You listening to me? You listening to me?"

Cobo tried to play it off but we all knew about the Replacement Center. It was for young guys on their way to adult prisons. Dudes got shanked up there all the time.

After dinner, which was creamed corn, corned-beef hash, rice, and lemonade, we had recreation and personal time. Mr. Cintron came over and said he got a letter for me, but the name of the writer wasn't on the list of people I could receive mail from.

"You don't have much of a list anyway," he said.

"All I got down was my moms," I said. "I had my friend Kenneth down, but they made me take him off. I had my brother Willis down, but they made me take him off because he was in here before and he ran with the Convent Avenue posse. That's all I got."

"You know somebody who spells their name *I-S-I-S*?" Mr. Cintron asked.

"Yo, man, that's Icy! Oh, man." I had to turn away because just mentioning her made me want to cry.

Mr. Cintron looked at me and told me to get up and follow him. I didn't want anybody to see me crying because they might think I was weak or something. I went into the office with Mr. Cintron and he told me to sit down.

"Who's this person?" he asked again.

"Her real name is Isis, but we call her Icy," I said. "When she was born my moms was just getting out of rehab and was doing a lot of reading on black stuff. You know, Egypt and Africa and stuff like that. And she named my sister Isis. She's nine and she's my heart, really. You know, Mr. Cintron, I really didn't think about her writing to me. But that's the kind of girl she is. Man, she's real good people."

"You want to add her name to your list?"

"Yeah, I do."

"So what's her last name?"

"Anderson. We all got the same last name."

"Okay, she's officially on your list. I can put the others back on, too. Here's the letter from her."

I put the letter in my pocket so I could read it later.

CHAPTER 3

Six o'clock in the morning and everybody was up. I heard Mr. Wilson making the rounds, calling out everybody's name. He thinks it's funny to call people names like the Godfather and stupid stuff like that. When he called out your name, you was supposed to yell out, "Glad to be here, sir!"

"Mr. Robinson the Terrorist!"

"Glad to be here, sir!" Play called back.

"Mr. Sanchez the bank robber!"

"Glad to be here, sir!" Diego called.

"Mr. Anderson the Vampire!"

"Glad to be here, sir!" I called to him.

"Mr. Billy the Kid!"

Toon didn't answer.

"Mr. Deepak the Serial Killer!"

Still no answer.

I heard Wilson go walking down the hall and then heard him on his walkie-talkie. Something had happened to Toon.

Wilson got us out and lined us up. When they took Toon from his room he was really messed up. His eye was all swollen and there was dried blood under his nose. Somebody had fucked him up bad. I guessed he was the youngest dude in the 3-5-7.

Wilson took Toon down to the nurse's station on the first floor. I felt real sorry for the dude, but I figured it was over and nobody else would mess with him. I tried to push it from my mind, but it wasn't that easy. Sometimes, when I get real mad, I can feel my neck swell up a little. I don't know why that happens, but it does. I took some deep breaths and tried to think about Icy's letter. She and her friend were going to enter a double-Dutch contest. She said she didn't think she was going to win but she needed the practice.

Thinking about Icy calmed me down. Some.

We had eggs and two little hard sausage patties for breakfast and the kind of potato thing they serve at McDonald's, but it was almost too hard to eat. Play said he was going to carry it around in his pocket all day and maybe the heat from his body would make it soft.

I was back in my room and checking everything for inspection when Mr. Pugh stuck his big head in.

"You like the breakfast you had this morning?" he asked me.

"It was okay," I said, not wanting to complain.

"Uh-huh. If we find out who beat up the Puerto Rican kid, we're going to have his ass on the menu for lunch," Pugh said.

"He ain't Puerto Rican," I said.

"Shut up."

Yeah.

"Everybody's in lockdown until 8:30 because we got some new equipment coming in," Pugh said.

We were on lockdown whenever there were strangers in the building. Play said that they were afraid that someone would tell us that Lincoln freed the slaves.

I wish I had said that.

Lockdown was cool. In my mind I knew I could deal with being alone. When I first got to Progress, it freaked me out to be locked in a room and unable to get out. But after a while, when you got to thinking about it, you knew nobody could get in, either. That was the cool part about being in Progress. You were in lockdown but you were also shutting the world out.

My cell is 93 inches long and 93 inches wide. The door is 32 inches wide and the window in the door is 22 inches wide. The toilet is at the far end, away from the door but near the front window, which looks out on a highway. If I fold my blanket up, I can stand on it and see cars going by or look down and see the fence with the barbed wire. Sometimes I like to look out at night and see the headlights and the red taillights from trucks as they pass. The window is closed tight and I can't hear them, but I can imagine how they sound.

Nothing moves in the cell except me. The bed comes out from the cinder-block walls, which are painted green. The closet is fastened into the wall at the end of the bed. From the window to the corridor you can't see much, but anybody can look in and see you whenever they want to, even when you're using the toilet.

I sat on the edge of my bed and took out my letter from Icy again.

Dear Reese,

How are you? I was thinking about you and I found a letter that Mama had written to you but didn't mail. It was a stupid letter anyway. Sometimes when I'm in bed at night I think about you and what you are doing. If you could think about me every night at exactly 9 o'clock, then we would be thinking about each other at the same time.

Jeni and I are going to enter a double-Dutch contest run by the church day camp. We can't jump that good, but I think if I get enough practice I'll be able to jump really good by next summer.

Everybody around the block is saying that the 4th grade is going to be soooo hard. You have x's in math in the 4th grade and you have to figure out what the x stands for. Mama is still sick. Luther came around and asked Willis if he could borrow $20. Willis said that Luther was the father and he should be loaning out the money.

You remember that old light-skinned woman who was living on the first floor? Her grandson got shot in the stomach. All he was doing was sitting on the stoop drinking some soda and there was some shooting across the street and one bullet came all the way over and got him. He was an innocent boy. He didn't die, but they don't know if he's going to be able to walk again. His name is Ghana.

Can you write back? I would like to get a letter from you.

Your sister,
Icy

CHAPTER 4

Out of lockdown. The light hurting my eyes. Me feeling stiff from the cot as I line up.

In class Diego was grinning and stuff, and the new kid, Cobo, was acting like he was down with everything. He started cracking on the teacher, Miss Rossetti. It was getting to her, and she told him that if he gave her a hard time she would put him on report. He gave her a mean look and I thought she looked a little scared.

Toon looked down at his desk all morning. There were minutes when I thought me and Toon were the same person. I was on the outside, dark and ready with my fists if anything went down, and Toon was the me on the inside, always a little nervous, always looking around to see what was going to happen to him. When dudes messed with Toon I felt they were messing with me. It didn't make a lot of sense, but it was something inside me.

We got this big colored cook named Paris, and at lunch he was slapping meat loaf on everybody's plate like it was steak or something. He asked me if I wanted some gravy on it and I said, "Yeah."

"You ain't man enough for no gravy!" he said. "Get out of here."

He was messing with me but it didn't mean nothing. The gravy was probably foul anyway.

Toon was in the mess hall when we got there. He looked real sad. But even when he was looking sad he looked like a cartoon. Play came and sat across from me. I saw he had some gravy on his meat loaf.

"Diego said that Toon cried when they were jumping him in," Play said.

"Shit." I knew that meant that he wasn't jumped in. "He's going to do him again?"

Pugh came by and we kept quiet.

The afternoon was one of them terrible ones. The air was real still, and whatever Miss Rossetti said sounded like *buzz-buzz-buzz*. I kept falling asleep and jerking my head up until she told me to stand up. If we had been in regular school I wouldn't have stood up, but I did because Miss Rossetti was okay. She wasn't trying to mess with anybody.

After school, group was canceled again, and we just sat around. Toon was in the corner by himself and Diego was laughing at him. Cobo went over and talked to Toon, and you could see Toon was freaking out.

Play was playing Ping-Pong with Mr. Pugh, but when it was just about time that we could turn on the television, he came over to where I was sitting.

"That new guy told Toon they were going to kill him because he punked out when they tried to jump him in," Play said.

"Get out of here."

"He told Diego to do him."

I looked up and saw that Toon had his face down in his hands. Toon acted kind of simple, but he never bothered nobody. I knew he didn't go asking if he could get into the 3-5-7, either.

Something told me to mind my own business, but I went over to where Diego was sitting.

"What you want?" he asked.

"Why you messing with Toon?" I asked.

"Why's it your business?"

"Toon ain't nothing but a kid," I said. "Why don't you leave him alone?"

"Why your breath stink so much?" he asked.

"It's from kissing your mama," I said.

He stood up and I stood up with him. We were like right on top of each other and he was bigger than me, but I was looking him dead in his eyes.

Pugh came over and stood right next to us, just like we were standing, except next to us he looked like a big-assed white mountain.

"The first one of you jerks to throw a punch I'm gonna kill, bury, and then piss on his grave," Pugh said.

"Why don't you kill the guy who beat up Toon?" I said.

"You the town snitch?" Pugh asked.

I turned and walked away.

"All of you are getting a little frisky today," Mr. Pugh said real loud. "You're all on lockdown for the rest of the day!"

When Wilson marched us to dinner, there were about nine white people sitting on one side of the mess hall with Mr. Cintron. There were two guys in suits sitting a little apart from them, and I figured they were guards. Pugh said we could talk if we kept the noise down.

"We supposed to be able to talk at dinner all the time," Play said.

"Shut up," Mr. Pugh answered.

The white people kept looking over at us, and I saw that Mr. Cintron was talking to them. They were eating something but I couldn't see what it was.

"Yo, Play, you thinking they eating the same thing we eating?" I asked, pointing to my two franks, sauerkraut, and mashed potatoes.

"If one or two of them curl up and die, then you'll know they got the same thing we got," Play said.

I saw Cobo go over past Toon and take one of his franks. I think Pugh saw it too, but he didn't say nothing.

Dinner is forty-five minutes, the same as the other meals. You could eat it in ten minutes but they give you forty-five anyway. Five minutes before the dinner period was over, the visitors got up and left. Mr. Pugh told us we had to wait until they were out of the building.

"Take five!" he said. "Smoke 'em if you got 'em!"

He knew none of us had any cigarettes, or at least we weren't supposed to have them, and he would report us if we did get some. We waited for twenty minutes past the end of dinner period before Mr. Cintron came back.

"That was a facility reform committee," he said. "They've got some good ideas, but they'll never come about."

"What kind of ideas?" Mr. Pugh asked.

"To put each young person with an individual tutor," Mr. Cintron said. "They figure it'd be more cost efficient than just warehousing these kids over and over. I'm supposed to fly up to Albany tonight and plead the case tomorrow, but I know the legislature won't spend the money for it. They're not smart enough. I'll be back by the afternoon with the bad news."

"Instead of that, you could get them individual tutors to kick their butts," Mr. Pugh said. He was laughing. If the legislature was made up of people like him . . .

When we left we saw the girls waiting in the hallway to come into the mess hall. They were pissed because they had been standing outside the whole time.

"We ate everything," Leon said. "That's what took us so long."

We got ten minutes of free time before they put us back on lockdown, and I knew that Toon would be safe for the night. But we wouldn't be on lockdown once Mr. Cintron got back. I told Play that I was thinking about telling Mr. Cintron.

"You can't be no snitch, man," he said. "You can't be no snitch."

I knew no one wanted me to be a snitch. Even the guards didn't respect anyone who passed along information. All we had were each other and sometimes you needed some homies, even if they were just temporary, to get by. Play was cool with me, but I knew if he thought he couldn't trust me then he'd have to walk away from me if anything went down.

I thought about writing Icy a letter, but I didn't want to write nothing stupid or just something about the joint. When I was first sentenced, she and Willis were in the court and the judge let me say good-bye to them.

"Progress doesn't sound too bad," Icy had said.

She was crying because she knew I was sad. Willis was telling me to be strong, and I was saying something—I don't even remember what—and looking around him to see if Mom was going to show. She didn't. On the way to Progress I imagined her waking up off a bad high and wondering what day I would be sentenced. No way she was going to say it was her fault she didn't show.

"Somebody must have given me the wrong date," she'd say with her proper way of talking.

I wouldn't write anything about Progress. The name sounded good and we were supposed to believe we were somehow actually moving in some direction, but it wasn't nothing but a juvy jail. From the way Mr. Cintron talked, it would get a lot worse if more kids were assigned to it.

I tried to sleep without thinking about Toon. What was happening was just happening. That's the way life was. Shit just came together, and if it rolled in your direction you got messed up.

What I knew, though, was that Cobo never did want no Toon in the 3-5-7. He was just the kind of gangsta fool who always went around looking for somebody to mess with. Luther was like that too.

Sometimes I think that's how he hooked up with Moms. She was weak enough to take him in and he was mean enough not to care about nothing except himself.

A month before I got arrested, he had met me on the corner of 145th Street, near where the bus depot was. He told me he didn't think I was his real son.

That was supposed to make me feel bad and it did. It hurt, but all I could think about was how I could get back at him. I didn't say it, but I thought it.

CHAPTER 5

We got up in the morning and it was lightning and thundering.

"In the old days," Pugh said, "they wouldn't execute a man during a lightning storm. Too dangerous."

I looked at the fool to see if he was serious. He was.

I saw Toon at breakfast and he looked the same. That stupid face he always wore, kind of round and wide-eyed with his hair sticking out all over his head, was looking more like a leftover pumpkin or something. The skin around his eye was yellow and blue, colors you didn't even expect to see on a real person, and the way he was holding his face when he was trying to eat his eggs, you could tell he was paining.

Diego and Cobo were sitting together. Cobo was still acting like he was some kind of big-time gangsta, and Diego was sucking up.

We finished breakfast, and Wilson said we had to wait until the girls came downstairs before we went to classes.

"They're getting a lecture on birth control," he said.

"All you got to tell them," Pugh said, "is to stay away from these knuckleheads."

We went to the dayroom instead of our cells, and I knew that the cells were being inspected as soon as Wilson left us. I thought about my place. I knew it was clean, so I didn't have anything to worry about. Anyway, you only got a demerit for dirt in your room, you didn't drop a level.

We were sitting around when I saw Toon go to the bathroom. Cobo snapped his fingers twice to get Diego's attention and then pointed at Toon.

"Diego!" I called to him. "Sit down, man."

Pugh looked up and then he looked at me and Diego. He knew something was happening.

"I think I'll get myself some coffee," he said.

Pugh was going to let the shit happen. He knew if I got into it, I could lose my gig at Evergreen.

"What you got to say?" Diego asked me from across the room as soon as Pugh closed the door.

I looked over at Play, and his eyes were dead on me, seeing what I was going to do. Diego couldn't handle me, I knew that. He looked strong but I didn't think he had the heart. But it wasn't Diego making the world go round. It was Cobo.

I went over to where he was sitting. He laid his head to one side and hooked his thumbs in his belt like I was some shorty he was watching on a playground. He was sitting on one of the folding chairs and had it tilted back. I kicked the leg and he went back onto the ground.

Diego took a step toward me, and Play stood up and pointed at him.

"You want him—you got me, too," Play said.

Cobo got to his feet, looked me up and down, and then the sucker just exploded on my ass! The sucker was hitting me with his fists, his elbows, kneeing me in my side. I was down on my knees covering up and he was pounding me on the back of my head. I was in a blind panic when I grabbed his ankle and pulled it up as hard as I could.

He started to go down backward and reached out to grab onto something, but there wasn't anything there. When he reached back for the floor he was all open, and I smashed his face as hard as I could. I don't remember a lot more but I know I kept swinging. Then I felt myself going up in the air and down hard on the back of the couch, which knocked all the wind out of me. Before I could see where I was, my hand was being twisted behind me and I felt the handcuff on my wrist.

I looked over my shoulder and it was Pugh.

He went over to where Cobo was trying to get to his feet and gave him a straight kick right in the stomach. Then he twisted his arm behind him and handcuffed him, too. Wilson must have heard the commotion, because he came running in. I got dragged out of the dayroom and pushed into my quarters. I heard the door slam behind me and just lay on the floor, still handcuffed.

I lay there for about an hour, maybe even two. Then Mr. Pugh, Mr. Wilson, and some other dude I didn't know got me out and took me to the detention cell.

The detention cell didn't have anything in it except a toilet. You had to sit on the floor. They brought me some water and a bologna sandwich later on and I told them to keep it. But I ate it when I got hungry.

I got another bologna sandwich for breakfast with a container of milk.

It was a long day, and I sat in the cell by myself until Mr. Pugh came and got me and took me to Mr. Cintron's office. I started to sit down but he made me stand up and face away from him. He got right behind my back and started talking to me real soft like any minute he might have offed me. I was thinking he was probably hard when he was on the streets.

"Anderson, do you have to work on being stupid or does it just come natural to you?" Mr. Cintron said.

"I ain't got nothing to say," I said. "I just did what I did."

"The guy you fought is going to be doing that same kind of fighting in some kind of institution for the rest of his life. And believe me, he's going to be in some kind of institution for the rest of his life. What the hell do you need that for?"

I tried to think of something to say, but I couldn't.

"Eddie said you were looking out for one of the

younger boys," Mr. Cintron said. "But I don't know if I believe him. All I know is that I stood up for you and you let me down. That's all I know."

"I'm sorry, sir."

"This isn't about sorry, Reese. You're not on the street stepping on somebody's sneakers. You're behind bars. You're with people who don't mind seeing you throw your life away. You can't figure that out?"

"Sir . . ."

"Shut up, Reese," Mr. Cintron said. "Just shut up. I'm going home tonight. Home to my wife and children and my lovely apartment and I'm going to think about this. You know what freaking power I have over you now? Do you know what—"

He just stopped talking like he was disgusted or something. I wanted to turn around to see his face, but I didn't.

When Mr. Pugh took me back to my quarters, he asked me if I was all right. I said, "Yeah."

"As soon as I turned my back you started acting up," he said.

"Yeah."

* * *

Dear Icy,

It was nice getting your letter. You made me feel a lot better. Sometimes it gets pretty bad in here, but I feel good thinking about you and Willis and the good times we will have when I get out. Do you remember when we went to Coney Island and you went on all those rides? That's the first thing we'll do when I get home. Tell Willis to save up a lot of money.

We have a real funny-looking boy in here. We call him Toon because he looks like a cartoon. He's only a little older than you are. I told him about you and he asked if you had a boyfriend and I said yes, you did.

Icy, I am going to try to get out of here as soon as I can so we can be a family again. I don't know the exact date, but I hope it's soon.

Your favorite brother,

Reese

I've felt bad in my life, but never so bad as when Mr. Cintron walked away. It was as if everything I had hoped for was gone. He had even put Icy on my mail list, and now I didn't know if I could send her the letter I had written. I remembered what she had written, to think about her at nine o'clock and she would be thinking about me. But I couldn't think about anything except that I had messed up again.

I wanted to see what the rest of the guys were thinking. There wouldn't be any talking at lunchtime, but maybe I could see something in their faces. That's what I thought, but Mr. Wilson brought my lunch to me and I had to eat it in my cell.

"Is that all you know?" he asked. "Settle everything

by fighting? Isn't that the kind of low-life crap that got you in here?"

"Yes, sir."

"You know, all Mr. Cintron has to do is to write you up and they'll send you right upstate with that kid you had the fight with. Then the two of you can fight all you want," Mr. Wilson said.

He looked at me like I was nothing, and that was the way I felt. But when he left, I thought about what he had said. Maybe he went home and dealt with his family and his friends like he wanted, but I had to deal with what I found at Progress.

I wanted to pray, but I don't like doing that kind of stuff. I mean, to me, praying sounds lame. You've messed up and then you go asking God to let you cop a plea. One time I heard Mama praying. She was in her bedroom and I thought she was praying to get off that stuff she was using, and I leaned against the door to hear her. But she was praying for ten dollars so she could buy some food. I knew what she would be buying with the ten dollars if she got it.

Mom was a trip and a half. She was small. I was as big as she was when I was nine. She was pretty when she fixed herself up. And she spoke well. Like

Icy. Icy probably talked like Mom, really, but when Mom spoke, you could hear every syllable. Unless she was high. And as much as I loved Mom when she was straight, that's how much I hated her when she was high. And she always tried to pretend she wasn't using when I knew she was.

But the main thing was that I knew how some of the chicks around the way copped their money to get high. You can finesse people in stores or you can finesse people in the post office, but you can't finesse no dealer. He knows what you need and what you'll do to get it.

Sometimes I dreamed about Mom and me and Willis and Icy living somewhere together, maybe in Queens, next to the park. It was a good dream when it started, but it never ended up good. Never.

The whole joint was quiet and I figured the staff had everybody on lockdown. Sometimes, especially if there was a fight or something, there would be a silent lockdown. You couldn't have a radio on or a television and you couldn't talk. That didn't bother me but it bothered some guys big-time. They had to have some noise going on all the time. I think maybe they were hearing stuff in their heads and wanted to shut it out. Those were usually the guys on the meds line in the morning.

When dinner came, I was glad to march with everybody to the mess hall. Dinner was the same as lunch, a hamburger patty, a slice of bread, some creamed corn, potatoes, string beans, and rice pudding. It didn't have any taste, or maybe I was just not up to tasting it, I don't know.

My light went out at eight thirty. I'm a level one and it wasn't supposed to go out until nine thirty. I wondered if Mr. Cintron had dropped me to level three, or even four. If I was on level four, I didn't get to go to school or have rec time. I wouldn't be going to Evergreen anymore, either.

Being at Progress, hearing the bars slam or standing in the halls waiting for somebody to unlock one of the steel doors, made me feel like maybe I was an animal or something. Going to Evergreen and seeing people walking around and smiling made me feel good even if they weren't smiling at me. They were feeling good about themselves, and that's what I needed.

The thing was that whatever happened to me, there was always something worse than there was before. The first time I was arrested, when they sent me up to Bridges on Spofford Avenue for two weeks, it was bad, but the worst thing that could have happened then was that I got a record. That was like a weight around my neck that was going to drag me down even further the next time I got into trouble. Then the last time I got arrested, I came here to Progress, which is a lot worse than Bridges. When Wilson said they could send me upstate with Cobo, I knew that would be even worse. If Cobo did have a gang up there, they would just probably kill me like they were thinking about killing Toon.

I guess dying is the worst shit you can get into.

Morning came and I got roused up with everybody else. We lined up and I didn't see Cobo. I was looking for him because he might be trying to sneak up on me and shank me or something. Play gave me a wink but Diego just looked away.

It was summer, and I knew school was out back in the world. My main dog, Kenneth, would be playing b-ball in the Fourth Street tournament. K-Man couldn't play a lot of ball two years ago, but now he was getting real good. Two teams wanted him to play in the Fourth Street tournament. I wished he could come up and visit me. K-Man is real people.

"Reese, out of line," Mr. Pugh said.

I stepped out of line, and he left-faced the crew and marched them off toward school. I was just standing there by myself but I knew better than to move. When Mr. Pugh gets mad at you, he can make your life two kinds of miserable.

He came back and told me to follow him. "Put your left hand on my belt and don't take it off!"

I put my left hand on his belt. And he started walking toward the staircase. We went to the stairwell and down the stairs real slow. Sometimes Mr. Pugh would stop and flinch like he was going to do something. I just held on to the belt. He was letting me know that any moment he could stop and punch me in the face. I was knowing it.

We went to Mr. Cintron's office. Miss Rice, his secretary, looked old. Mr. Wilson said she had been working at Progress for over fourteen years.

Mr. Cintron came out of the office and he told Mr. Pugh to bring me in.

"You want him handcuffed to the chair?" Mr. Pugh asked.

"Yes," Mr. Cintron said.

He went around to the other side of the desk while Mr. Pugh cuffed me to the chair and left. Mr. Cintron shuffled through some papers and shook his head like he was disgusted.

What I was thinking was that if I went upstate and they were going to kill me, then it would be better if they did it right away. I didn't want to have to walk around looking over my shoulder all the time.

"We picked you!" Mr. Cintron said, looking up at me. "We selected you for the work program because you had a high IQ, you hadn't done anything violent, you had a decent reading score, and you sounded like you really wanted a break. So everybody on the board is going to be looking at the 'model' for this work project and making a judgment. And you're here getting into fights. You really know how to screw things up, don't you?"

"Sir, I'll break my back to make it up," I said. "I'll do anything you say. I'll work hard, I won't get into any more fights. If somebody wants to beat me up, I'll just let them. I swear it, sir."

"Hey, you've already proven that your word doesn't mean shit," Mr. Cintron said. "So why are you giving me that bull now?"

"I'm giving you the only thing I know, sir," I said.

"I'm not a snitch, sir, but they were talking about offing Toon. I just didn't want that to happen, sir."

"Reese, well, maybe we were wrong about your IQ," Mr. Cintron said. "You're in here with boys who can steal, who can shoot each other, who can kill. That's the kind of life you chose, and that's the life you got. And you're one of them. So when you start running down some bull about you couldn't let this happen or you couldn't let that happen, it doesn't mean a thing to me. You stole because you didn't want something to happen. Deepak—the boy you call Toon—is in here because he wouldn't behave himself. Tell me where I'm wrong, Reese. Tell me where I'm wrong."

"You're not wrong, sir," I said. "I was wrong, but . . ."

"But what?"

"I was just wrong."

"So, I have a number of options," Mr. Cintron said. "The first is to write up a report on the fight and give you a nice label. How about 'Aggressive and violent. Cannot control temper'? Then I can send in the report and have you transferred to an upstate facility. You ever been to one of the long-term facilities? In New York they usually put them in nice areas upstate. It's pretty up there this time of year. You can fight up there to your heart's content. They have a half dozen gangs and you'll be in one of them, and then you can get ready for your visit to Manhattan. You ready for that?"

"What's that?"

"That's when they send you back to the streets for a visit," Mr. Cintron said. "It's only for a visit because you'll blow it again and be back in some facility. You're lucky you didn't get a longer sentence."

"I can't get another chance?"

"I don't want to give you another chance, Mr. Anderson," Mr. Cintron said. "But if I take away your chance, if I report this incident, that our 'high-IQ, nonviolent, carefully selected choice' has messed up, it's going to stop the work program in its tracks. Why should we fund this program, pay the extra insurance, and pay for the extra staff hours if these *African Americans* are just going to throw it away? They're going to look into my face and talk about recidivism rates and emotional instability and social understanding—but in their hearts they're going to keep it a lot simpler. They're going to be thinking that people like you don't deserve a chance.

"So I'm going to squelch this report. I'm going to

let Maldonado, the other kid, take the whole blame," Mr. Cintron said. "Not for you, because I don't have any faith in little punks like you, but for the next kid who comes along and might deserve it. So you're going to continue in this program, Reese. But if you screw up again, you'd better send your soul right to God, because your black ass will belong to me and I will put a hurting on you. Am I making myself clear?"

"Yes, sir."

"I'll find the worst facility in the state to send you to and warn them about you," he said. "And if I do that, you'll be sorry as long as you survive." He pressed a button on the intercom and said, "Mr. Pugh, get him out of here."

Mr. Pugh uncuffed me. When I stood up, I almost fell down, my legs were shaking so bad. Mr. Pugh took me back to my quarters and told me to wash the floor, and I started doing that.

The soapy water was cold and wasn't getting the floor clean, but I was down on my knees scrubbing it the best I could. I was crying but I wasn't making any noise.

The thing was that I didn't know if I was going to mess up again or not. I just didn't know. I didn't want to, but it looked like that's all I did.

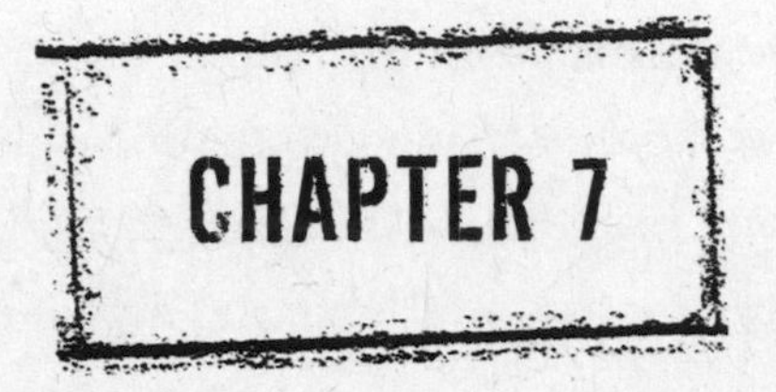

CHAPTER 7

"You sweet on Toon?" Mr. Pugh had me in a Ripp belt with my hands handcuffed to it in front of me. At least I was in the passenger seat of the van instead of the back.

"Why I got to be sweet on him because I don't want to see the dude killed?" I asked. "You want to see somebody killed?"

"I seen guys get killed," Mr. Pugh said. "In Iraq I seen our guys get killed and a lot of Raqs running off to meet Allah."

"That was war," I said. "This ain't war."

"Yeah, whatever. He didn't ask you nothing about me?"

"No."

We drove the rest of the way to Evergreen in silence. I knew what Mr. Pugh was thinking. He could have lost his job if Mr. Cintron knew he had split from the room when he saw what was going down. I wasn't going to rat Mr. Pugh out because I knew he could do a lot more to me than I could to him.

We got to Evergreen, and he parked the van and came around to my side.

"You're doing okay," he grumbled at me. "Don't mess it up."

I wasn't really doing okay. Mr. Cintron had been in my corner and now he wasn't. He'd made that clear, but he'd also said he wanted me to make it happen for all the juvies who were going to follow me. I liked that.

Father Santora was in the lobby when we got there, and he came up with this big smile and reached out to shake my hand. I couldn't shake his because Mr. Pugh hadn't uncuffed me.

Once I was uncuffed, Mr. Pugh said he would be by to pick me up at four, and then Father Santora sent for Simi. She came down and he told her to have me working on the rest floor.

Simi was short and brown skinned. It looked like

all the help at Evergreen were colored and the residents were all white. She had a little gold tooth on one side of her mouth. It looked a little strange, but she had a nice smile.

"I have a cousin who looks just like you," Simi said as we walked up the steel stairs. "Only he's got good hair."

"That's nice," I said, which sounded stupid even before it got all the way out.

The rooms on the rest floor looked a little like our quarters at Progress. They weren't small but they weren't huge, either. Each room had a bed, a sink, a chest with drawers, and a smaller room, about the size of a closet, with a toilet. They also had at least one window, which was cool. The beds were the kind I had seen in hospitals. If you pressed a button, the head or foot would come up.

Some of the rooms had oxygen tanks in them. We had an oxygen tank at Progress in the nurse's office.

Simi, who looked okay, kind of Spanish and kind of black, gave me a big plastic bag and told me to go to each room and collect any garbage they might have.

"Six rooms. We had patients in seven rooms but

Mr. Cloder died," Simi said. "You get used to that. All of these people here are very old. After a while they die and you say amen and you move on. After you collect all the garbage, then you go and you stay with Mr. Hoof. He's not feeling good and he might need some help. Anything he wants you to do, you do it."

"Which one is Mr. Hoof?"

"Can you read?" Simi asked.

"Yeah."

"Okay, so when you go into the rooms, you look at the nametags on the inside of the door. When you see one that says Mr. Hoof, then you know who he is. All right?"

"Yeah."

"And knock before you go in, even if the door is open," Simi said.

My conversation with Mr. Cintron kicked back in and I wanted to impress Simi with all the work I was going to do. I wanted to impress Mr. Hoof, too, but I didn't know who he was yet.

I went to each room, knocked, and when whoever was in the room asked me what I wanted, I said I was supposed to collect the garbage.

"Why isn't Simi doing it?" a man asked me. The

name on his door read GONDER.

"I don't know, sir," I answered. "She just told me to do it and she's in charge of me, so . . ."

"Don't take my newspapers," the man said. "Sometimes I read them over to see if I've missed anything."

"I do that sometimes too," I said.

"Where do you live?" Mr. Gonder turned his head as if his neck was stiff.

"Just past the Bronx," I said.

"Where past the Bronx?" he asked.

"Near the warehouses," I said, not wanting to tell him I was at Progress.

"You should move to Harlem," Mr. Gonder said. "They're fixing it up nice. My uncle lived there years ago when it was a really good neighborhood."

"Oh."

"I don't think you live up there," Mr. Gonder said. "You look like you're from Brooklyn. You from Brooklyn?"

"No, sir."

"I can tell where people come from by the way they talk, too," Mr. Gonder said. "They got a certain way of talking in Brooklyn. I don't like it."

"Yes, sir."

Mr. Hoof's room was the last one I went into. I saw his name on the door but it wasn't *Hoof,* as I thought—it was *Hooft.*

"Hello, sir, I came to collect any garbage you have," I said.

"Where's the colored girl that was doing it?"

"She's in charge of me," I said. "And she told me to collect the garbage."

He was sitting on a chair near the window. He had a book in his lap and I thought it might be a Bible. I found a newspaper on the floor and asked if I should throw it away.

Mr. Hooft motioned with his hand and I put the paper in the plastic bag. He looked really old and thin. His face was white but he had a lot of dark marks on his cheeks that looked like birthmarks. I thought maybe he had a disease.

I finished picking up the stuff in Mr. Hooft's room and took it out to where Simi was sitting at a desk in the hallway. She asked me if I had any trouble and I told her no. She took me to a closet at the end of the hall, opened it, and told me to tie the top of the bag up tight and then put it in the closet.

"The cleaning staff picks it up at night and puts it out for the waste disposal people," she said. "So what do you think of Mr. Hooft?"

"He's okay, I guess."

"He's nice once you get to know him," she said. "Come on, I'll give the two of you a formal introduction."

I thought that was cool. I also noticed that Simi knocked on the door even though Mr. Hooft saw us coming.

"Hello, Pieter," she said. "I want you to meet Reese. He's here from the Progress Facility and he's going to be working ten days a month for us. We think he's going to do a marvelous job."

"What's the Progress Facility?"

"It's a place for young men who have made a mistake," Simi said. "But I think Reese has learned his lesson and now he's on the right road. Aren't you, Reese?"

"Yes." My heart sank when I saw Mr. Hooft's face. He was looking over at me as if he was scared of me.

He beckoned Simi over and pulled her next to him. I heard him say that he didn't want me in his room.

Simi straightened up. "Mr. Hooft, you'll have to

work with whatever staff we have. Reese is a very intelligent boy and he will be working with us. Now you two get acquainted, because he's going to be assisting you with keeping your room clean, with your personal hygiene, and anything else you need. He's a very good young man."

Simi patted me on the arm and walked out of the door.

Mr. Hooft looked at me and then looked toward the door as if he might have thought about getting up and running. I saw a cane in the corner of the room, so I knew he wouldn't be running too fast.

For a while we were silent, me standing in the middle of the floor and him sitting by the window looking at me. I tried to think of something good to say.

"Is there anything I can do for you, sir?"

He got up slowly and I thought he was going to leave the room, but then he went into the little bathroom. I didn't know if he was going to stay in there, maybe lock himself up or what. There was a stool near the chest, and I went over and sat on it.

I hadn't been around a lot of old people before and I didn't know how to act. There had been a program on television about teenagers robbing old people. Maybe he had seen that and was getting spooked. Simi had told me to stay with him, so I just sat on the stool.

After a while the door opened and he came out and looked around the room like he was wondering if I was still there. I stood up and he looked me up and down.

Then he went back to his place on the chair.

"You murdered somebody?" he asked me.

"No, sir," I said. "I didn't murder anybody."

"White or black person?" he asked. He had an accent.

"Sir, I didn't murder anybody," I repeated.

"You're in jail now?"

"Yes." I didn't like saying I was in jail. I remembered when I first got to Progress I began thinking about what I would say to people when I got out, what I would call the place.

"You raped a woman?"

"No, man. I didn't rape a woman and I didn't kill anybody."

"So what did you do?"

"I would rather not say."

"Simi!" Mr. Hooft called out. "Simi!"

"Sir, please give me a chance," I asked him.

"What did you do so terrible you can't even say the words?" he asked. "Simi! Simi!"

Simi came to the door and looked at me and then at Mr. Hooft.

"What happened?" she asked.

"This man, is he a murderer?"

"No, he is not a murderer, Mr. Hooft." Simi put her arm around my waist. "He's a very nice young boy."

"If he was a very nice young boy, he wouldn't be in jail," Mr. Hooft said.

"Sometimes, Mr. Hooft, people make mistakes," Simi said. "And Reese will be working with you."

She left again and I saw that Mr. Hooft had got his cane and was leaning on it as he sat. He was breathing kind of heavy. Then he turned his head toward me.

"So what did you do?"

"I needed money real bad," I said. "I knew this one guy, Freddy Booker, who hung out on my block, was dealing prescription medicines. He was getting homeless dudes to go to certain doctors and get prescriptions for painkillers and Viagra and things like that. They would give him the prescriptions and he would give them, like, two dollars apiece or something like that. Then he would get the prescriptions filled and sell the pills on the street. He would buy any kind of prescription that was either sex medicine or painkillers.

"I knew where this doctor had a storefront office. It was in a rough neighborhood and usually closed at night. I know it was wrong, sir, but I broke in and stole a whole bunch of blank prescription forms. The ones with the numbers on them. I sold them to the guy who was dealing prescription drugs.

"What happened then was this same guy was busted for dealing with a doctor downtown on 127th Street."

"In Brooklyn?"

"No, in Harlem."

"Then what happened?"

"When he got picked up, he snitched out everybody he knew, including me. They charged me with about eighteen counts of dealing drugs and unlawful distribution and stuff like that, everything the guy was charged with. I copped a plea to doing just what I did, and that's how I got to Progress, sir.

"But yo, like, I'm trying to turn my life around and I'm not going to do anything like that again. That's for sure."

"I don't like colored people," Mr. Hooft said. "Nothing personal, I just don't like them. And you're a colored criminal and I don't like criminals, either."

"Right." I had been standing up but I sat back down again. I knew if Mr. Hooft said anything negative about me, said I sassed him or anything, it was going to go against me, so I just shut up. Even if it wasn't true, it didn't matter. I was a criminal, like he said, and what really went down didn't matter all that much.

"Did you know the doctor?"

"No, sir," I said.

"But you stole from him anyway, and this other person, the one you were working for—what was his name?"

"Mr. Hoof, I wasn't working for him—"

"Hoof*t*! With a *t*. Colored people can't say that? P-i-e-t-e-r Hooft!" Mr. Hooft said. "Simi can't say it and you can't say it. There are certain things in your makeup which make you who you are. You coloreds steal and use drugs and you kill people and you can't even pronounce a name. Your brains are bad. That's why you were slaves."

What I would have liked to do was to hop to this sucker and beat his head in, but it would've been the same as beating my own head in, because I would be the one doing the most suffering. I didn't feel I was letting what he said slide, but I held back from saying what I really felt.

When Mr. Pugh came to pick me up, I was ready to go back. He asked me if I had had a nice vacation.

"I was working," I said.

"What were you doing?"

"Picking up garbage," I said.

"Good job for you," Mr. Pugh said.

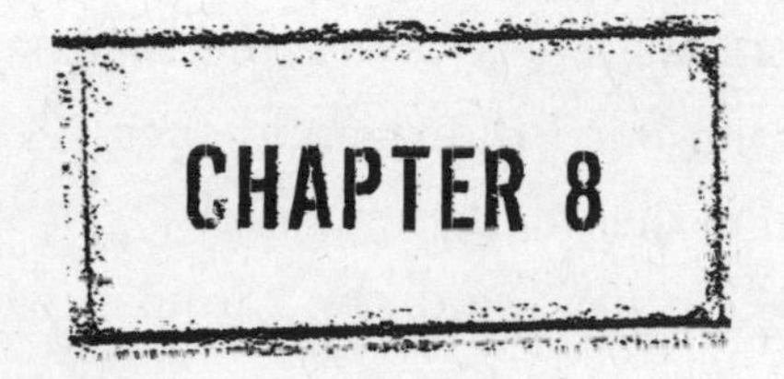

CHAPTER 8

At Progress you could get visitors any day between 10 in the morning until 4 in the afternoon, and on Saturdays and Sundays between 10 and 6 in the afternoon. I hadn't had any visitors, so when Mr. Wilson called me out of the dayroom Sunday afternoon I thought it was a mistake.

"Who is it?" I asked.

"Your mother and sister," he said with a grin. "I might have to steal your little sister, she's so cute."

I stopped dead in the hallway and looked at Wilson to see if he was kidding. My moms hadn't visited me in months. "You sure?" I asked.

"Yeah, it's for you. Remember, they can't give you anything to bring into the facility," Wilson said.

"They're supposed to leave all gifts at the office."

"Yeah, okay."

The visitors' room was decent. There were red and yellow tables you could sit at and real curtains on the windows. There were cameras in each corner of the room, but I didn't mind them. A television was tuned to the weather channel.

I looked around and saw a woman who looked like my mom standing in front of one of the vending machines. She was alone. For some reason I thought for a moment she might not recognize me.

"Hey."

My mother turned and looked at me and smiled. She was looking neat, maybe a little thinner than the last time I saw her.

"Well, how you doing?" she asked.

"I'm okay," I said.

She kissed me on the cheek. "You're taller!" she said. "They must be feeding you good."

"The food's okay," I said.

We sat at one of the tables. "They said that Icy was with you."

"She's in the bathroom," Mom said. "So what's going on?"

"Ain't nothing going on," I said. "I'm in here doing the time."

"I tried to get your father to come up," she said. "He said he was tied up and maybe he would get up the next time."

"Yeah."

"He's so far back in his child-support payments I can't even keep track of them," she said. "I got a date to take him down to Family Court and he didn't show. They don't do anything, so I don't know why I keep getting dates."

Out of the corner of my eye I saw Icy come out of the bathroom. She came over with her hands on her hips doing her movie-star walk.

"Reesy, darling!"

"Yo, Icy!" I got up and she threw her arms around me and hugged me harder than I thought she could. "Let me look at you, girl."

Icy stepped back and put her hands on her hips and turned around.

"Yo, you sure you're nine or you're nineteen?" I asked.

"What were you doing?" Icy asked, slipping into a chair at the table. "I bet you were playing video games."

"I don't think they have any video games in here," I answered. "How long it take you to get up here?"

"We got the bus at twelve thirty," Mom said. "But I bet it stopped in every little place that had a convenience store or a gas station. My back is killing me."

"You should try riding the van all the way up here," I said. "When I came up, the scenery was nice, though."

"They got a school," Mom said. "I saw it in the brochure. You learning much?"

"Learning I don't want to be up here," I said.

"We're learning how to divide fractions in school," Icy said.

"You going to summer school?" I asked.

"If I go to summer school, then I can get into Harlem Children's Zone." Icy squinched her eyes up and wiggled the way she does when she's pleased with herself.

"They're not taking you just because you got a half a dimple," I said. "You got to have something in here." I tapped her on the head.

"I got smarts going on," she said. "And now that I heard the good news, you know I'm going to study hard."

"What's the good news?"

"Hillary Clinton is not going to be the president, so that leaves the door open for me to become the first woman president," Icy said.

"They giving out GEDs?" Mom asked.

"You can take the course or you can apply for the tests," I said.

"'Cause you know you got to be doing something with your life when you get out of here," Mom said. "You know that, right?"

"Yeah, I know it," I said.

There were two other families in the room. One was a girl's family and the other one I recognized as Play's aunt and cousin.

"Did you look into any of the family programs they have?" Mom was still talking.

"Like what?"

"You're just going to do your time and then slide on out to the streets again?" she asked.

"I'm going to school," I said. "You don't have any choice. Even if you have a high school diploma or a GED, you got to go to school unless you're on some kind of medication where you can't learn anything."

"You can learn if you put your mind to it," Mom went on. "If you don't put your mind to it, then naturally you won't learn anything. I don't want you coming home and just hanging out. . . ."

She was starting to drone on, talking about the value of education like she was inventing it or something. She came up to visit and she was sounding like a recording or a television commercial. I knew she didn't care about what she was saying, either.

I checked out Icy and she was looking around, scoping what the inside of a jail was like. Jail wasn't the visitors' room and I knew Icy was getting the wrong impression, but I didn't want to say nothing.

". . . they have programs at the Family Resource Center down on Worth Street to help keep the family together when you get out." Mom was still talking. "You know anything about them?"

"Not really," I said. "They down there and I'm up here."

"I left some papers for you to look at in the office," she said. "They aren't that hard to read."

"Yeah, okay."

Her skin was dull and her eyes were a little watery. I wondered if she was using again.

"So if you run for president, what's going to be

your slogan?" I asked Icy.

"Okay, I got the whole thing figured out," Icy said. "I'm going to tell everybody that they can get free food. In school we learned that the average family of four can be fed for seven thousand dollars per year, okay?"

"Go on."

"I need you to write a letter for me," Mom said.

"Let me finish telling him this, Mama," Icy said.

"We can't stay all day, girl!" Mom snapped at Icy.

"You just got here," I said.

"I'm starting a new job tonight," she said. "I'm going to be working as a waitress at Sylvia's."

Lie.

"What kind of letter?" I asked.

"Reese, I'm really worried about your brother," she said. She put her hand on mine. "I think he's running the streets too much. He's either going to get himself killed or end up in jail."

"He knows what he's doing," I said.

"I don't think so," Mom said. "In a way I think he's looking up to you instead of the other way around. You're in jail now, so he thinks it's cool or something. I'm trying to get him to go into the army and do something with his life. Learn a trade or even make a career of it. You know what I mean?"

"Plus he'll get an enlistment bonus. The man told us," Icy said.

"And he can use that for his college education when he gets out." Mom shot Icy a glance.

"So you can feed a family for seven thousand dollars. . . ." I looked back at Icy.

"Are you hearing me?" This from Mom.

"Yeah."

"So I want you to write Willis a letter telling him that you think it's a good idea for him to go into the army before he gets into trouble," Mom said.

"Yeah."

"No *yeah,*" she said. "Do it! I don't want to see both of you in jail."

"Okay, I'll do it," I said.

"Where's the bathroom?"

Icy pointed it out to her, and she got up and walked away.

"What you thinking?" Icy asked me when Mom was going into the bathroom.

"Tell me about your campaign for president," I said.

"You didn't tell me what you were thinking," Icy said.

"That's 'cause you're too ugly," I said, tapping her on the wrist.

"Anyway . . . so there are a hundred and ten million families in the country. So to give them free food every year will cost us seven hundred seventy billion dollars. That sounds like a lot but it's really not that much. If you're in a war, you can spend that much in three years. So my campaign is that you give everybody free food for four years—"

"While you're the president?"

"Yeah."

I loved my sister's smile.

"And then what?"

"Then they would be fed for four years, we couldn't afford to pay for a war, and people could turn their attention to doing stuff for themselves and be happy."

"Okay, you got my vote," I said.

"Can you still vote if you go to jail?"

"Not while you're in jail," I said. "I don't know, really."

"How do you think Mom and I look?" Icy asked.

"You look fine," I said.

Mom came back and said they had to go. "I don't

want to mess this job up," she said. "I figure if I'm making money and can help Willis, he won't be stealing or anything."

They weren't there but a minute and then they were gone. If they hadn't come at all, it would have been cool, but just to blow in like that and then blow out was hard.

"You headed back to the dayroom?" Wilson asked.

"Can I sit here a minute?" I asked him.

"Yeah."

I sat for a while trying to think why I was feeling so bad. I was in the facility and I couldn't go home and I was feeling lonely, but there was more to it. It was like I wasn't connected with nothing in the friggin' world. Nothing.

Play's people were hugging him and I saw them leave. Then I watched some more people come in. Indian people. A man and a woman. They were kind of heavy and they sat in a corner. After a while Wilson came in with Toon. He went over and sat with the Indian people and they started in on him. Toon had his head down.

"Look at what you are doing! This is a disgrace!"

the woman was saying. "Look at where you are!"

I knew Toon felt bad. I felt bad for him. Parents were supposed to be loving us, not telling us about how we were disgracing them.

I looked up, saw Wilson near the door, and went over to him.

"Can I hang in the dayroom awhile?"

"Sure, man."

We went out of the visitors' room. I took my clothes off and he searched me for contraband. Then I dressed and went back to the dayroom. They were watching *Cops* on television.

Her name tag read Karen Williams, but all the guys were checking out the short skirt the woman was wearing. On the blackboard behind her she had written "Exit Strategy" in big letters.

"So, who knows what an exit strategy is?" she asked.

"That's how to get out of here," Play said.

"It's how to get out of here in a way that means you won't be coming back," Miss Williams said. "Or does anybody here want to come back?"

Nobody answered the lame question.

"One of the things you want to have in hand is either a GED or a head start in taking the GED exam," she went on. "Employers want to see what you have accomplished in life, and one way of showing them is to have your GED."

"What they know most from that is that you didn't finish regular high school," Diego said. "That puts you on a whole different level than kids who finish high school with a regular diploma."

"I think it shows initiative and a willingness to work," Miss Williams said.

"But they know you ain't in the top set," Play said. "If I was going for a job, I wouldn't be waving my GED in front of anybody unless they asked me for it. And what they mostly ask you is if you've been arrested or anything."

"Which is illegal," Miss Williams said. "They can't ask you if you've been arrested, and if they did ask, you don't have to answer. Did you know that?"

"Did you know that if you don't answer, they won't hire you?" Play said. "And if you go and make a complaint, all they got to say is that they were thinking about hiring you in a job that handles money and you had to be bonded. Then they can ask you anything they want."

"A lot of what you're saying is true, but that's why we have courts, to fight abuses," Miss Williams said.

She had her legs crossed and we all took a look. Not bad.

"So you got your GED," Diego said. "Then they're going to want to know what you've been doing for the last year. You tell them that you've been in church, see—"

"Redecorating the confession box," Leon said. "Putting in a tile floor like they do on television."

"Yeah, yeah," Diego went on. "Then your probation officer gives them a call to see how you doing. Or he comes around with a little cup for you to pee in. Then the job is gone because everybody knows where you've been."

"Okay, a lot of what you're saying is true," Miss Williams said. "On the other hand, if you show up with no high school diploma, and no GED, how does that help?"

"At least you won't be disappointed when they turn you down," Leon said.

Some of the guys laughed. I looked over at Toon. He wasn't laughing.

Miss Williams kept on talking but it wasn't coming through. What all the guys knew was that there was a world on the outside and we didn't belong in it.

Maybe we could get over once in a while, but we really didn't fit in.

When the session was over, Miss Williams handed out a form that listed all of the papers we were supposed to have once we got out. That was cool, because whenever you go someplace, you have to start all over again or they turn you down for something because you don't have the right papers.

The right papers didn't mean anything. You were still yourself in your own black skin and you couldn't sound like some white dude or some la-dee-da black dude who was heavy into what was going down with education or being middle class.

My moms had left the papers for me to sign, but when I took them to Mr. Cintron and he was telling me how cool the family program was, I saw that she could get some money from it and figured that's all she really wanted. That's what I thought. And Icy had given me the 411 on Willis going into the army. The enlistment bonus. If he got that, Mom would try to con him out of it. That's what she was about.

I wondered if she had been different at one time. Maybe she even thought about being the first woman president. And then, maybe, things just started happening that turned her around. I felt for her, but I wished she was stronger, someone that me and Willis and especially Icy could depend on.

After group skills we went to the B wing to get our teeth checked. While we were waiting, we sat with some new guys and one girl. The orientation flick was on television. The new kids were looking at the TV screen, but out of the corners of their eyes they were checking us out. I saw Diego trying to look hard.

Diego, in my mind, was a punk. But his head was so messed up that he was a dangerous punk. Every morning between breakfast and school he was on the med line. I had seen a lot of the guys do that, but I couldn't figure out how they knew who needed the pills. The nurse gave them one or two pills in a small cup, and another cup filled with water. They took the pills and then drank the water. Then she made them stick their tongues out and move them around so she could make sure they swallowed the pills.

The dentist was white with dark hair and big eyes and this sincere look on his face. He asked me how often I brushed my teeth and I told him once a day.

"Why not twice a day?" he asked.

"I don't know, man," I said.

"It only takes an extra two minutes a day," he said.

"Okay, I'll try it," I said.

He thanked me and told me it would be worth it. I had never seen anybody get into teeth before. But two minutes a day made sense.

At dinner one of the newbies sat across from me and Play. He was my height but wide and ugly. Sucker looked like King Kong with a nappy 'fro and a jumpsuit.

"Where y'all from?" he asked.

I didn't say nothing and Play didn't say nothing. The newbie started puffing up like he was mad and asked us again where we were from. We still didn't say nothing, mostly just because he was a newbie, and he picked up his knife from the table and held it in his fist. That cracked me up a little because it was just a plastic-ass knife.

"I just came in from your mama's house," Play said. "She told me to tell you hello."

The guy looked at us like he was ready to go off. Then he said that he was from the Duncan Avenue projects in Jersey City.

"We kill a guy just for smiling at us," he said.

I got up and went to another table because I really didn't want to fight the sucker. Play got up with me, and we sat with some white dudes from the Special Attention wing. Those were dudes who were all messed up and were in the special watch-these-guys-because-they-might-hurt-themselves area in the back of the classrooms. One guy we sat with didn't look up from his tray. The other guy put his hands, palm down, over his plate like we were going to take his food.

Toon needed to be with these guys.

When we finished eating and Pugh lined us up to go back to our wing, King Kong came over and got behind me.

"Me and you got some business to take care of," he growled at me.

I thought back on what Mr. Cintron had said. All these dudes in here had run stupid until they found the front door of some courthouse, and half of them were still running on empty.

"You think you can kick his ass?" Play asked me later.

"I don't know if I can kick his ass," I said. "But if the deal got to go down, I can sure make it a war he didn't want to be in."

Lights-out and I was lying in the dark thinking that King Kong was going to get both of us screwed up. I wondered if he knew it too.

CHAPTER 11

So what happened is that Mr. Pugh brought me a candy bar and talked to me decent on the way to Evergreen. I don't like people giving me nothing, but I took it and said I would eat it later.

"So, you looking forward to going home?" he asked.

"Yeah."

I wasn't sure. I knew I didn't want to be in Progress anymore, but I wasn't sure what home was going to mean. Just the way King Kong was messing with me, I knew the streets were waiting to mess with me. All my homies hanging out and dealing whatever they had were waiting, all the suckers leaning against the rail on the corner and looking to see who was weak were waiting, and all the gangbangers with nothing to do but cook up some mad were waiting. Yeah, home.

The papers Mom had left were about some program that New York City was running. They said that anybody who was accepted for the program would be eligible for help in getting affordable housing and more money on their Family Cards. I knew it was all good on paper, but in real life it didn't go nowhere. In a way all the programs were alike. If everything worked out perfectly, you should be doing okay. But the deal was that you were going back into the same hole you had slid down before. It was like Toon. His people talking about how he had messed up and how embarrassed they were and him sitting with his head down thinking that the best thing going for him was to get out and go back to the same family. I could see him wanting to stay at Progress.

CHAPTER 12

It was raining when I got to Evergreen. I had gone to class from 8 to 8:30 and King Kong had sat behind me. He kept bumping the back of my chair. I felt like turning around and lighting him up, but I knew all I had to do was get into one more fight and my game would be over.

I was cleaning up some soup in the hallway that had been spilled by one of the residents when a real dark sister came over to me.

"What you doing, cute boy?" she asked.

"Who are you?" I asked.

"Nancy Opara from Nigeria," she said. "I'm an exchange student and I work once in a while here for extra credit."

"You don't get paid?"

"I get extra credit from Saint Elizabeth's," she said. "Simi told me about you. She said you were nice."

"I'm okay," I said.

"I think I'm going to recommend you for mayor of New York City," she said. "The city needs a nice young mayor."

"I think that job would be too hard for me," I said.

"All you got to do is to hire a lot of smart people to work under you," she said. "You don't have to know anything yourself."

She was kidding around with me and I liked it. At Progress nobody kidded around with you. Even when you were talking to your friends it could change in a minute. You said the wrong thing and somebody would get mad and swing at you, or they were having a bad day and you didn't know it, or their medication wasn't working. You could never tell.

When I was collecting the garbage, the seniors looked at me careful but they didn't say nothing. I figured in a couple of weeks they would start thinking of me as somebody who worked for Evergreen. That's what I wanted to do, to fit in and be nobody special.

After I collected the garbage, I went in and

cleaned up Mr. Hooft's room. He wasn't there when I first started cleaning, but then he came in. He was slow getting up on his bed and I thought maybe he wasn't feeling good.

"Good morning, sir," I said.

He didn't answer.

His room was clean to start with and I finished pretty quick. "You need me to do anything else?" I asked.

"What are you thinking?" he asked.

"I'm thinking you might want me to do something else and I can get it done," I said.

"You don't like me?"

"I guess you okay," I said. In my head I was thinking, *No, I don't like you.*

He picked up his paper and started reading it, and I sat down on the chair in the corner. He looked over at me and asked me again what I was thinking.

"Why you got to know what I'm thinking?" I asked.

"You could be thinking of stealing something from me," he said. "You see that soap dish in my locker? It's solid silver. Go ahead, look at it."

I looked in his locker, saw something shiny, and

picked it up. It was a soap dish, like he said, with a little scene on the top part. Some kind of birds under a tree.

"It's nice," I said, putting the dish back into his locker.

"So you're thinking of stealing it?"

"Mr. Hooft, I didn't even know you had the dish," I said. "I was thinking of this guy who wants to pick a fight with me. He keeps messing with me, but I know I need to maintain my cool so I don't get into trouble. I can control myself, so it's okay. I don't think about stealing or nothing like that, because that won't get me anywhere."

"He wants to fight you in jail?"

"Yeah."

"That happened to me once," he said. "You want to hear how it happened?"

"It ain't the same because you weren't in jail," I said. "I'm in jail, and whatever you do against the rules gets you into trouble. It don't matter who's right and who's wrong. You fight, you're in trouble."

"You don't know nothing!" Mr. Hooft said. "When I was a boy, nine years old, my family lived in Java. You don't know where that is because your people don't know anything, but it's in Asia. Maybe two thousand miles from Japan—"

"How you know my people don't know anything?" I asked.

"Why are you interrupting me?" Mr. Hooft asked.

"Why you can't speak to me like I'm a man, same as you are?" I asked. "I'm not putting your people down."

"The nurse said I don't have to take nothing from you!" He was turning red. "One word from me and you are out of here!"

"Yeah, that's all good, but you don't need to be insulting me."

"I can't bother with you," Mr. Hooft said. "I have to change my bandage."

He had a bandage on the outside of his right leg up near his hip. He gave me a mean look and got up on the bed, took the tray of bandages from the white cabinet next to his bed, and lay on one side with his back toward me.

I sat down and watched him pull the old bandage off. It might have hurt him, but he didn't say nothing. Then he just lay there for a while, breathing heavy.

His butt was hanging out but he really didn't

have a butt, just a crack with a little flesh on it. Seeing his naked skin, I didn't think he even looked real. More like a bad drawing or something. I had never seen many butts and I didn't like seeing his.

What I thought I should do was just walk out of the room and come back when he was finished. Instead of that I watched as he tore open an envelope and took out a piece of gauze and tried to put it on his leg.

"You want me to do that?" I asked.

"You're a nurse now?"

"I can move around better than you can," I answered.

"Just put the gauze on and cover it with a piece of tape," he said.

He had a hole in his leg. I didn't want to look at it.

"I got to go talk to Simi," I said.

"What do you have to say to her?" he was asking as I left the room.

I found Simi and told her what I had seen. "He got a hole in his leg about this big." I made a circle with my fingers around the size of a quarter.

CHAPTER 13

Simi led me back to Mr. Hooft's room. He had covered himself up with the sheet and she threw it off and looked at the hole. Then she went out of the room.

I looked at Mr. Hooft and he wasn't moving. I knew he wasn't dead, but he was lying still. When Simi came back, she had a small tube of something.

"This is not going to hurt, Mr. Hoof," she said, still leaving off the *t* from his name. "It's just an antibiotic. I'm going to get Reese to change this bandage whenever he comes. I'll change it the other days."

She looked over at me and nodded for me to come watch.

What she did was to put some antibiotic on the

hole, then take out a piece of gauze, roll it carefully, and place it right over the hole. Then she pulled the hole together a little and taped it shut.

When she left, I sat back down again in the corner. I didn't like seeing nobody messed around like that. Even though I wasn't liking him, I didn't want to see the hole in his leg.

"You want to hear what I was telling you that happened to me?" he asked.

"Go on," I said.

"My family lived in Java. My country owned all of those little islands before the war. My father was a schoolteacher. Very tall. We're a tall people. My mother was a seamstress at home, but when she married, she settled down to being a housewife.

"My father was offered the position of headmaster in a rural school outside of Surakarta. He planned to work there for two years as headmaster, and then return to Europe to teach. But then the war broke out. First it was the Germans and then the Japanese. Nobody thought it was going to last because nobody took the Japanese seriously. In December 1941, they attacked your country. Then in 1942, they overran Dutch Indonesia.

"We heard rumors and more rumors and I was afraid, but Mama kept telling me that everything would be all right. Then one day some Japanese soldiers showed up in our garden. There they were, sitting in our garden with their long rifles, and we were having breakfast inside. They came and took Papa away and searched the house. We had nothing in the house except books and papers. Then they left. Three days later they came again and took Mama and my sister and me to a camp. We stayed in that camp for months, and it was terrible. There wasn't enough food and we were all living one on top of the other one."

Mr. Hooft was turning in his bed and winced when he got around on his bad leg.

"You want me to call Simi again?" I asked.

He shifted onto his back and waved his hand in the air.

"But then one day they came and got all the boys and took us to a different camp. There were people crying and screaming and women fighting to hang on to their boys. You know why? You don't know why. Because there was talk of some of the men being killed. They said that the Japanese soldiers shot some of the men, and some they made them kneel on the ground and then cut their heads off."

"I don't believe that," I said.

"Why?" Mr. Hooft asked. "Why don't you believe it?"

"I never heard of it before," I said.

"Do you know about the Dutch East Indies?" he asked.

"No."

"Do you know about Martin Luther?"

"Yeah, Martin Luther King," I said. "He made that 'I Have a Dream' speech."

"No," Mr. Hooft said. "Your black Martin Luther King was named after Martin Luther—a German—who lived many years ago and who was also a religious leader. You don't know anything. That's why you're in jail."

"Fuck you."

"So when they rounded up the boys and took us to another camp, we were all terrified. The Japanese soldiers were very scary because they had dark skins—not as dark as you—and they were short. They were no bigger than we were, and we were only boys.

"But they swaggered around and they had guns. And anything you did they would punish you. Sometimes the punishment would only be a slap. Sometimes they would tie you to a fence and beat you with whips. Sometimes they would take boys away and we wouldn't see them again."

"They cut their heads off?"

"I don't think so. There were even stories that some of the youngest boys were taken to Japan," Mr. Hooft said. "But I know we never saw them again. Anyway, there was one boy in the camp I was taken to who seemed to hate everyone, but especially me. It was as if he had the soul of the devil.

"I was thin and not used to having to defend myself. When he found me—that's the way I thought it was, him finding me—it was as if he had found an answer to all of his problems. He would torment me day and night. We were given a ration of boiled barley every morning, and he would come and take mine. The other boys would see him coming and eat as quickly as possible, but I would be so petrified I would just sit and tremble."

"He punked you out," I said. "You were too scared to deal."

"I don't know exactly what you are saying," Mr. Hooft said. "What I know is that I was afraid of the Japanese. If we had a fight, I knew the Japanese would take us away and punish us. They would beat us up and maybe even kill us, and he knew it too."

"He knew that?"

"Of course he knew it," Mr. Hooft said. "He saw what the rest of us saw. But for some reason he lived on the very edge all the time."

"So what happened?"

"So after a while, maybe ten months to a year after the Japanese took over the island, and all the boys and some of the older men were in this one camp, we settled into a routine. Every morning we would have to go up the road—maybe two miles to where the men were working—and we would sit outside the gates until the guards led the men away on work details. Then we would have to go into the camp and find the dead bodies and load them onto trucks."

"The dead bodies?"

"Men died from being weak, from disease, from whatever," Mr. Hooft said. "At the time I didn't know what dying was about. But I didn't want to touch the bodies. When someone died, they tied them in cloth and put them in baskets. Then we had to lift the baskets onto the trucks. If you got the legs it wasn't too bad, because the legs weren't too heavy. The legs went up first, and then the boy carrying that end would run around and help push the basket onto the truck. But it was from the other end that the liquids came out. That was terrible, because it stunk and it would get on you and you would smell terrible all day. That's what dying meant to me, the smell. This boy, he wouldn't push the basket with the others, and then maybe the whole basket would fall on you.

"One day he and I were pushing a basket onto a truck and he moved away. I struggled as much as I could but then it fell back on me and I was on the ground and trying to catch my breath. He was a boy like me, but when he came over, he looked gigantic. His face was wide and big and he was kicking me like he had so much hate for me. His hate scared me more than the pain from his foot. I was lying on the ground. Did I fight back? I don't know. I knew it was hopeless, that we were fighting against different demons. Two guards came up and started kicking me and they knocked him down. He was bleeding and he wouldn't get up, and they kept beating him and beating him. Later that day me and another boy had to carry him in a basket for the next morning's crew."

"That really happened?" I asked.

"It happened," Mr. Hooft said. When he said it his voice changed, got very high and very soft, almost like a kid's voice. I wanted to look at his face, but he was half turned away and I could only see the thin outline of his cheek and his right eye. "It happened."

When Mr. Pugh came and got me, he asked me how I liked my vacation. I thought about telling him what Mr. Hooft had told me, but I didn't think he would have understood it.

CHAPTER 14

The stuff that Mr. Hooft said was scary. For some reason I just didn't want to deal with it, but it stayed on my mind. Maybe Mr. Hooft thought I was like that guy fighting him, or maybe even one of the soldiers. I didn't know.

On the way back to Progress I remembered Mom saying I should write to Willis. I didn't want to but I knew she would keep bugging me. Me and Willis weren't all that tight, but he was still blood and would get my back if I needed him. He would get Icy's back too. But he was steady going to thug school and making noises like he was too fast for the streets to catch up with him. One time when my pops wasn't being too stupid, he said the streets were like quicksand covered with whipped cream. You knew when they were slowing your ass down, but it always came as a surprise when you got sucked under.

In the rec room they had some paper that had PROGRESS printed on it so that it looked like a private school or something. I copped a few sheets and wrote to Willis.

Dear Willis,

Mama came up to the jail with Icy. I don't know how Mama is doing but I was glad to see them. She asked me to write you a letter and say you should join the army. What she said was that being in the army would keep you off the streets and turn you away from getting into trouble. I was going to write f'd up but you can't put anything like that in a letter from here.

Anyway, I know there is a bonus if you join and I guess either you or Mama would get it. If she tells you that she's going to hold it for you I don't know what to say.

In a way she is right that being in the army would get you off the street. I don't know if you remember Guy from the Bronx. He lost thirty-two pounds to get into the army and then he went and got killed in Iraq. He was a hero and they had a special service for him at Mt. Olive. But after the funeral and everything he was still dead and nobody said anything about him that sounded special to me. He went into the army, he was killed, case closed.

So, in a way what I am saying is where you think you wouldn't mind dying? If you died while you were in the army it would go over big on 116th Street but it wouldn't mean much on 125th because that street is jumping too heavy to care about just another soldier dying.

Mama said she would like to see you join the army because it would keep you safe. How's it going to keep you safe if there's a war on?

I talked to an old white dude who was in one of those wars with a number on it. Maybe they should put numbers on all wars just to see how many they got going and how stupid it looks. If you went all the way back to Bible times it would probably be up to War 302 or something.

The bottom line is that you got to look out for number one, which is you. I know that might seem funny coming from me writing to you from jail. I don't know if I would join the army unless I could learn a trade that would get me a good job when I got out. Maybe I could learn to drive a tank and come back and take over everybody's parking spot in the hood.

If you don't mind dying here in Harlem then that's another deal, because ain't nobody except me and Icy going to make a big thing over it because it's really not that unusual. Some people would put R.I.P. on their windshields or something to show love, but I don't know how much love you can show to somebody dead.

So what I'm saying is that maybe you need to be thinking about getting to some place where people aren't even talking about dying. When I get out of here I got to chill for a few years until I can figure out a way to get paid. I'm not into no quick get overs because I'm tired of being locked up. I was thinking about you and me opening a business. Maybe we could open a grocery store and be like the kind of guys who everybody in the neighborhood looked up to. We could even open up a supermarket and hire some guys from the hood. Icy could go on to college and maybe run for mayor of New York, and you and me could get all the people in Harlem to vote for her. The newspapers would run stories about why people should vote for some black girl from Harlem but then Icy would come out and blow everybody away with her plans to make New York the best city in the world for everybody (not just for white people) and she would be mayor. I bet that would even straighten Moms out.

Anyway, Moms asked me to write to you but I can't say nothing too heavy because I don't really have anything useful in my pocket right now. As you know my situation is definitely not all that tight, either.

Write back if you get a chance.

Your brother,

Reese Anderson

Saturday. Miss Dodson from ACS—Administration for Children's Services—and Miss Rossetti from Progress announced that instead of our regular Saturday routine we were going to have a basketball game and then a co-ed group session.

Miss Dodson handles kids in the foster system, and I figured that had to be a hard road because they didn't have a home to go back to when they got out.

"Remember they did the same thing before Christmas?" Play asked. "We're supposed to be smiling and stuff when we play."

"Yeah, first they divide us into two teams and run the game," I said, remembering the Christmas program. "They video the game and then the whole group thing is about how basketball is supposed to be about life."

"What they call it again?" Play was eating an apple. "A semaphore or something like that."

"A metaphor," I said. "Remember Miss Dodson asked us to show how basketball was like life, and that kind of girly dude said that the ball was round and life was round, and she asked him what that meant and he said he didn't know but he had noticed all balls were round."

"That guy was a goof," Play said.

"Why you eating the core of that apple?" I asked. "You that hungry?"

"No, I'm too lazy to take it over to the garbage can," Play said.

Miss Rossetti set up the teams with me, Toon, Play, Mr. Pugh, and a skinny kid who was on some serious meds on one side. On the other side they had Mr. Wilson, Diego, Leon, a fat white kid everybody called Lump, and the King Kong dude who was messing with me before.

My team was the shirts, and when King Kong took off his shirt I saw he had a bird tattooed on his chest with some Chinese writing on it.

He said that it was his name in Chinese letters and that his name was Tarik.

"That's why it's got five letters," he said.

"You know I read Chinese," I told King Kong. "And it don't say no Tarik."

"What it say?" He looked at me sideways.

I got real close and squinted at the letters. "It says, 'Please flush after each use.'"

Mr. Pugh and Play cracked up, and Mr. Wilson put his hand over his mouth. Everybody was laughing but King Kong Tarik.

The game started and the only real ballplayers on the court were me, Play, and Mr. Wilson. Everybody else was jive. Mr. Pugh was running around knocking people down and walking whenever he got the ball. Me and Play were scoring; all we had to do was to keep the ball away from Mr. Wilson.

Toon was a trip. If he had the ball and you came near him he'd give it to you. We'd be waving for him to pass but he'd panic and give the ball to anybody near him.

When I got into the low post, King Kong kept coming over to me and leaning his body against mine like he was digging me or something. I put my elbow in his chest a couple of times and told him to back off. He knocked Toon down a couple of times even when Toon didn't have the ball. He wouldn't mess with Play and he tried to goof on Mr. Pugh, but Mr. Pugh was so busy with whatever he thought he was doing he didn't even dig it.

When it went wrong I didn't even notice it right away. All I know was that King Kong gave Toon an elbow to the back of his head and I automatically did what we did in the hood when some big jokey fool started hitting people on the court. I stomped down on the top of his foot near the ankle.

He grabbed at his leg, then he jumped up and came toward me. I thought he was going to chest me up but he didn't. The sucker lit me up! He was throwing a lot of punches but he really wasn't hitting all that hard.

Mr. Pugh grabbed him around the waist and pulled him off me. I put my hand on my mouth and saw my lip or something was bleeding.

"Calm down! Calm down!" Mr. Pugh was yelling. "This is only a freaking basketball game! Calm down!"

I looked over at King Kong, and he was breathing

hard and running me up and down with his eyes like he was ready to kill me.

"Are you calm now?" Mr. Pugh had both arms around King Kong and was yelling into his ear.

"Yeah, yeah!" King Kong said.

It wasn't really me, but it was somebody in my skin taking a step forward and hammering that fool in his temple with the side of my fist.

Sucker's arms went up into the air and he flopped down on the ground.

"Everybody here is on report! Everybody here is on report!" Mr. Pugh was screaming.

Okay, so what happened was that Miss Dodson was only there for the day and we were supposed to have group. Mr. Pugh and Mr. Wilson wanted us all back in our cells and locked in, and they were going to figure out if anybody had to go to detention. But Miss Rossetti came up with the idea that this was a perfect opportunity to teach us something in group.

The story was that everything was up to Mr. Pugh and Mr. Wilson. I figured Mr. Pugh didn't care one way or the other and would follow whatever Mr. Wilson wanted to do. If Mr. Wilson was mad, then me and King Kong would probably be written up and both of us on our way to 23-7. If I went to 23-7, then Mr. Cintron would definitely tear me up. If Miss Rossetti could get Mr. Wilson over his mad, I had a shot.

We were lined up and taken to the dorm hall, where we had to stand at attention with our hands in the "perp" position, behind our backs as if we were cuffed, for fifteen minutes. Then Mr. Wilson came and got me and King Kong and took us into one of the 23-7 rooms.

"What you guys need to learn?" he asked. "That these steel bars will keep your dumb butts calm if you can't control your dumb-ass minds? That's what you need to learn? Or if the steel bars don't slow you morons down, you know what will? That little chalk mark they put around your body in the street. What's your pleasure, girls?"

"He started it," King Kong said.

"I didn't mean to start nothing," I said. "I was just having fun."

Mr. Wilson leaned close enough to me so I could actually smell him and spoke softly into my ear. "Your life ain't about fun," he said. "It's about holding enough of your ass together to walk free again. You understand that?"

"Yes, sir."

"If either of you so much as cross your eyes in group, I'm going to nail you to a wall just like they do those bear skins," Mr. Wilson said. "We're trying to give you a chance to make something of your ugly selves because that's our job, and we'd like to turn you around so you don't mess up our lives with your bullshit. But don't think for a minute that it's personal, because it's not. Any of you mess up, we'll nail you, send you to the next lockup, and move on with our lives and the routine here like you never even existed. Do I make myself clear, Mr. Anderson?"

"Yes, sir."

"Do I make myself clear to you, Mr. Sanders?"

King Kong said he understood.

But when we were leaving, King Kong gave me a look and screwed up his face. Sucker didn't understand nothing.

"So why do you think I put the chairs in a circle?" Miss Rossetti asked.

"So we can check out the girls?" Diego asked.

There were two girls at the group session, Kat and Eileen, a black girl who worked in the nurse's office sometimes.

"Because circles are nonthreatening," Miss Rossetti said. "And the girls aren't here to be 'checked out.' At this session we're going to see how brave everyone is. What I want us to do is for anyone to start, and tell us two things that they're afraid of."

"What's brave about that?" Play asked.

"Well, let's find out," Miss Rossetti said. "Would you like to start?"

"I ain't afraid of nothing," Play said.

"Everybody has fears," Miss Rossetti said. "I think we can all agree to that. Anybody else want to give it a try?"

"I'm afraid anytime I leave Alphabet City," Diego said. "You can let your mind wander—you know, thinking about your woman or something—and step into another gang's turf. Then you end up getting shot or stabbed or beat down just for not paying attention. That's one thing I'm scared of."

"So you're afraid of street violence," Miss Rossetti said. "Would you like to say anything more about street violence? Are you only afraid when you leave your neighborhood?"

"Yeah, more or less," Diego said. "When I'm on my block, my boys got my back and I know I'm cool."

"If your boys really had your back, you could walk anyplace you wanted to and nobody would mess with you because they'd know there would be some comeback." King Kong was looking smug.

"Comeback ain't doing me no good if I'm being wrecked," Diego said. "You thinking I'm going to be up in heaven looking down and getting happy over some comeback?"

"Diego, if you die you ain't going to heaven," Play said. "Suckers like you die and go to Walmart.

They got a storage area in the back for dead punk-eros."

"We don't need to make this personal," Miss Rossetti said. "And we won't. I think that neighborhood violence is something to be afraid of, especially when you're young."

"Another thing I'm afraid of is getting caught up in a stickup or a drive-by with some fool who don't know how to use a gun just popping off caps and killing everybody," Diego said.

"More neighborhood violence," Miss Rossetti said. "And the thing to remember is that violence doesn't stop affecting us when we get behind closed doors. The threat is always there in our subconscious. Do you agree?"

"Not really," I said. "Unless some dudes are outside your door and trying to get in."

"That doesn't hold true for everyone," Miss Rossetti said. "And people do handle their fears differently. How about you, Deepak?"

Toon looked up when he heard his name. He smiled, shrugged, and folded his hands. "I'm afraid . . . sometimes I'm afraid, but not all the time. . . ." He looked around and sort of half smiled.

"Sometimes I'm afraid that my father will be disappointed in me."

We waited for him to go on, but he didn't.

"We have expectations of ourselves," Miss Rossetti said. "And people have expectations of us and sometimes we worry, as Deepak said, about how we measure up."

"You got a little saying for everything we're afraid of?" Play asked.

"Well, I've been thinking about this for a long time and a lot of people have done studies on adolescent fears," Miss Rossetti said. "And although I have some insights, I think we all can look at the problem of fear and come to some conclusions. Don't you think so?"

"I guess," Play answered.

"Anything else, Deepak?" Miss Rossetti asked.

"Sometimes I think my mother will be mad at me," Toon said.

Miss Rossetti nodded slowly. She looked around the room and then held out her hand toward King Kong.

"Mr. Sanders?"

"I ain't afraid of nothing," King Kong said. "I

can handle my business and everybody knows that. Anybody even act like they want to mess with me, I'll go to work on their ass."

"So you're afraid that people might mess with you?" Miss Rossetti said.

"No, I ain't."

"Ladies?"

"I'm afraid of losing my child," Eileen said. "When I come up here, my case manager was talking about how she didn't know if I could be a good mother and then she was talking about how my baby could be put with a responsible family. I had a girl friend who went away for eighteen months and . . ."

Eileen started crying and turned her head away. We waited a few minutes for her to get herself together, but she didn't say anything else. Miss Rossetti looked at me and gave me a little smile.

"I don't know what I'm afraid of," I said. "You know, like you say, everybody's afraid of something and I guess I'm afraid of something too, but I don't know what it is. Maybe getting old and dying. That don't look cool."

"I'm a little afraid of that myself," Miss Rossetti said. "My mother lost her memory when she got up in years and, quite frankly, that frightened me a lot. I even dreamed that I was losing my memory."

"So they put her baby with this couple—they were like black middle class"—Eileen had started again—"and then when my friend came home they didn't want to give the baby up. She said that Family Services put pressure on her too."

"Was she working when she came home?" Miss Rossetti asked.

"No, she was having some trouble. She was using again, but all she needed was some time," Eileen said. "I don't want to lose my little girl. She's all I got."

"I can understand that," Miss Rossetti said.

"You got kids?" Eileen asked.

"No, I don't," Miss Rossetti answered. "But I can imagine how it must be to have someone in your life you love and then have them taken away."

"Another thing I'm afraid of," Eileen said, "is being in a fire. I'd rather be in a drive-by than in a fire."

"Have you ever seen anyone who was injured in a fire?" Miss Rossetti asked.

"No. I don't want to see it either," Eileen said.

"How about you, Miss Bauer?"

"I'm not afraid of anything," Kat said. "The only

thing you have to be afraid of is people, and I'm not afraid of people because I don't care about dying."

"I think everyone has a secret fear of dying," Miss Rossetti said. "We imagine—"

"I'm not afraid of dying!" Kat cut Miss Rossetti off. "The guy that got me in here thought he could threaten me and tell me what he was going to do to me, but where is he?"

"I think we need to take a deep breath, Miss Bauer," Miss Rossetti said.

"He's dead because he tried to use me like he wanted to use me, and that wasn't going to happen!" Kat was looking fierce with her mouth all tight and going pale. "If you're not afraid of dying, then you're not afraid of anything! And I don't need to take no deep breaths because I'm not afraid of restraints, either."

That was the end of group because everybody saw that Kat was going off big-time. Miss Rossetti broke us down and she went with the boys back to our dorm, and Mr. Wilson and the lady guard went with Kat and Eileen back to the girls' wing.

CHAPTER 17

Our cook, Griffin, gave us broiled franks, sauerkraut, mashed potatoes, peas, juice, ice cream, cookies, and fruit for lunch. Broiled franks are like a hundred percent better than boiled franks. It was like we were at a ballpark or something and having real life instead of prison life.

"Griffin must have hit the lottery or something!" Diego said.

"Maybe they're going to execute us this afternoon and this is our last meal," Leon said.

I wished I had said that.

Play said when he got out he was never going to have franks again.

"Every time I look at a frank it reminds me of my

life," he said. "Ain't nothing to it."

I knew how he felt and I told myself that I wasn't going to have franks again either.

In the afternoon the maintenance crew was cutting down some trees and we tried to have a class but it didn't work. With the windows open it was too noisy, and with the windows closed everybody was falling asleep. Mr. Wilson wanted to know if we wanted to play ball or just hang out in the dayroom until supper. I didn't want to do either, but I ended up in the dayroom watching television.

I was checking out what was on the tube, but my mind was back in the group thing we had had. People were talking about what they were scared of and I knew that it wasn't for real. You didn't just come out and start laying out your program to people like that. You had to say something cool, which everybody did. Except for Toon. Toon was afraid that his parents weren't going to like him. I remember them yelling at him on visiting day, and when I played it back in my head I remembered they were looking around to see who was checking them out. They wanted everybody to know that they were better than Toon. I wondered if my moms thought she was better than me.

I was most afraid that my whole life was going to be about being in places like Progress. I had heard about people going to jail, getting out for a minute, then just going back. One teacher told us that for some people, being in jail was better than being free because you got "three hots and a cot." That was bull, but I could see how easy it would be to mess up again. Willis was on the street. I knew he could get caught doing something any day. On the street, you did anything to get over. If you had something going on, maybe some college or if your family had a lot of money, then maybe you could follow a good path. But if you didn't have nothing going on, then it was going to be hard just to squeeze yourself from one day into the next.

Mr. Pugh said that most guys ended up coming back. I didn't like his ass, but I thought he was probably right. My bid wasn't too heavy, but I knew how easy it was to get a ton of time if I blew it again.

Play came over and sat near me. He was looking across the room and shaking his head like he does sometimes when he's mad.

"Yo, Reese, Diego and Sanders are getting their heads together," Play said. "I think they planning on starting something."

I scoped out King Kong and Diego talking. Diego lifted his head, like he could feel my eyes on him or something, and stared at me. I gave him the finger and looked away.

"If they start something, I got your back, man," Play said.

Play talked hard, but I had never seen him do anything. I thought he was in my corner, but that didn't mean anything unless he was going to stand up when the bell rang.

Mr. Wilson came over and sat near us.

Me and Play bumped fists and went back to watching some girl on television saying that her ex-boyfriend was her baby's father.

"Now why would she get on television and lay out her business like that?" Mr. Wilson asked. "I think that's stupid and demeaning."

"And *what*?" I asked. "It's stupid and *what*?"

"Demeaning," Mr. Wilson said. "That means it makes you look bad. Don't you think she looks bad talking about how she's going with one guy now but she went with this guy a year ago and he's the baby's father?"

"Yeah," Play said.

"But the guy running around the stage like he did something to be proud of," I said. "He's smiling and going on."

The guy was saying the baby couldn't be his because he had a big head and the baby had a little head and his nose wasn't right. The whole thing was sick, but it came to me that it wasn't real, either. It was like they were putting on a play and everybody was supposed to be entertained.

Play laughed at the guy and the girl, and Mr. Wilson laid out his serious lines as usual. I was just thinking that I had to sit and watch this crap because I didn't have anything else to do in Progress but watch the time go by. My life wasn't any more real than those clowns on television.

My lights were still going out at eight thirty, and I was lying on my bed when Diego came to my door.

"You hear the news?" he asked. "Deepak is going to fight Sanders this weekend. It's all arranged. That little Indian is going to be killed."

They were setting me up. Diego knew I had defended Toon before when Cobo got on him. Now he was fixing it up between me and King Kong.

I told myself I didn't care. If Toon couldn't handle his business, that was on him.

I thought about telling Play to see what he would do, but in my heart I knew Play had to be pushed too hard to make a move. I couldn't get to her, but Kat was the person I really needed.

Really, Toon needed Kat.

CHAPTER 18

When I got to Evergreen Mr. Hooft was sitting in his room. A mask covered his nose and mouth. He looked at me and didn't say nothing and I didn't say nothing. Something had happened and I guessed he needed help breathing. The mask was attached by a tube to a little machine sitting on the table next to his bed. The machine made a low hissing noise that was louder when Mr. Hooft was breathing. Sounded like Darth Vader.

I sat in the corner and didn't stare at him or anything.

There were some magazines on the end of his bed and I wished I had one, but I didn't want to just ignore Mr. Hooft or act like I didn't care what was happening to him. I also had a letter that Mr. Cintron gave me in the morning just before I left for Evergreen. The letter was from K-Man. I had had time to read it before I left, but then I got worried that K-Man was going to say he wasn't my friend anymore and just put the letter in my pocket.

After twenty minutes or so Nancy Opara came into the room and took the mask off Mr. Hooft and asked him how he was feeling.

"I don't like that thing!" he said.

"The doctor said you had to wear it to assist with your breathing," Nancy said. "You don't want to put a strain on your heart, do you?"

"That machine puts a strain on my brain!" Mr. Hooft answered.

I liked that.

Nancy took Mr. Hooft's temperature and blood pressure and wrote them down on his chart. Before she left, she told me that I looked like I was Hausa.

"Do you know the Hausa people in Africa?" she asked.

"Tell her you're an American!" Mr. Hooft said.

Me and Nancy laughed, and she left.

"So, Mr. Big-Time Criminal, who did you shoot

today?" Mr. Hooft asked me.

"You know I didn't shoot anybody," I said. "Why you on my case, anyway?"

"I'm just interested in knowing how the criminal mind works," Mr. Hooft said.

"My mind works just like yours," I said.

"How can your mind work like mine?" Mr. Hooft leaned back in his chair. "I'm not a criminal. You are the one in jail. Keep that in mind."

"Yeah, well, you were in jail once," I said.

"It was not a jail," Mr. Hooft said. "It was a children's camp and it was during the war. Entirely different. With you there's no war on, and you people like to shoot each other and fight. That's what you do, right?"

I shrugged and thought about King Kong. "Sometimes you can't help it," I said. "If somebody wants to fight you then you get stuck in it."

"Why do they want to fight you?"

"Didn't you tell me that this guy in your camp wanted to fight you?" I said. "Why did he want to fight you?"

"I don't know," Mr. Hooft said. "Maybe he lost himself. Sometimes people lose themselves and then they do funny things. It happened in the camp. Sometimes they would stand up and scream. Maybe they would run around naked. I don't know. He was in the camp and as lost as the rest of us. We stopped knowing who we were."

"How you stop knowing who you are?"

"You know your name," Mr. Hooft said. "You look in the mirror and you see your face, your eyes staring back at you, but what does it all mean? Are you a man? One time a man was somebody strong and big, but who are you when you are not strong anymore? Not big anymore? Are you a father? A grandfather? But what happens when your children walk away? When they don't come to see you? Are you a father if you don't have a son?"

"You losing me, man," I said. "I don't understand what you're saying."

"It doesn't matter." Mr. Hooft waved his hand in the air. "In the end it doesn't matter. All that matters is that I keep my eye on you. You never let a hoodlum get behind you, so I have to keep you in front of me at all times."

"I'm not a hoodlum," I said.

"You probably have one of those guns they have

in the Middle East," Mr. Hooft said. "Those automatic guns. Yes, that's what you people like. Shoot as many people as you can real quick."

Mr. Hooft nodded to himself, and I knew he was enjoying messing with me. The room was pretty neat except for some papers on the floor and I picked them up and put them in the garbage can. The can had a plastic lining, and after I had picked everything up I removed the lining and took it out to the big trash can in the hall closet.

When I got back Mr. Hooft had got up on the bed and was pulling the sheet over his legs, which were really skinny and white.

"You know, there's a guy at Progress that always wants to fight me," I said. "You think he don't know who he is?"

"Where is he?"

"Progress," I said. "That's the name of the jail I'm in."

Mr. Hooft leaned forward and spoke in a low voice. "That's the jail? And they call it Progress?"

"I guess they don't want to call it just plain jail," I said.

"But *Progress*?"

"They got to call it something," I said.

"They have all young people like you, or they have older men, too?"

"From twelve to sixteen," I said.

"This boy, he doesn't like you?"

"I don't think he likes anybody," I said. "He's just a jerk."

"You think the Japanese will kill you if you fight him?"

"There aren't—that's stupid," I said.

"Don't you like to fight?"

"I can take care of myself," I said. "I'm not afraid of this dude, man."

"Look at you, puffing up like a bird," Mr. Hooft said. "The two of you are finding yourselves."

"So this guy died and the Japanese let you out?" I asked.

"The war ended," Mr. Hooft said. "It ended as horribly as it began, with bombs. When I went home to the Netherlands I was a hero. My family treated me like a king. I was young when I left Java, and so most of my life I was celebrated. I came to America when I was twenty and only worked important jobs because I knew who I was. You'll never find out anything, because you have more muscles than brains in your head. And you have a very round head. Did you know that?"

"My head isn't that round," I said.

"Do you drink tea?"

"Tea? Yeah, sometimes."

"When you get out of jail and I get out of here, you can come to my house and maybe we'll have a glass of tea together," Mr. Hooft said. "And you can teach me to be a hoodlum."

"Yo, man, you know I'm not . . ."

He turned away from me and looked toward the window.

"When I get out maybe we can hook up," I said.

Mr. Hooft didn't look at me, but he nodded. I finished straightening up the place and after a while I could see he was asleep.

Nancy looked in. "You do a nice job for a Hausa boy," she said. "Sometimes Hausa boys are lazy."

Mr. Pugh was five minutes late in picking me up. He searched me, which wasn't necessary, and found K-Man's letter, which he said he was going to confiscate.

"Mr. Cintron gave me that letter just before I left the joint," I said. "So you need to clear it with—"

He smacked me hard across the face. Case closed.

I thought about what Mr. Hooft had said about the kid in the children's camp fighting him even though the Japanese didn't allow any fighting. The bully paid for that fight with his life. But I didn't know about him trying to find himself. I didn't even know how to figure out if you could lose yourself. At home, out in the world, everybody knew where they were and mostly where they were going.

I was handcuffed in the back of the van. I knew I was going back to Progress. I knew one day I would be out and going back to the streets. I was scared that one day after that I might be headed back to Progress or another jail like the predictions everybody was throwing at me. In my hood, that's what happened. We all saw what was going down, but why it was going down was harder to get to.

Mr. Hooft's talk about getting out of Evergreen was strange. It almost sounded like he was in lockdown the same as me.

CHAPTER 19

Mr. Pugh gave me my letter from K-Man after he searched me again. I wanted the letter to be full of good news about the neighborhood and especially about him. It wasn't.

Dear Reese,

How are things going? Did you get a date yet? I saw Icy and she said she visited you. I asked her how she liked the place you were in and she said it was okay, that nobody could get in and get you. I thought that was funny.

Bunny's brother got shot. You remember his brother Vincent? He's got dark skin but a patch of white on his neck? Vitiligo—that's what it's called—and I wouldn't want to have it for nothing in the world because people stare at you. Anyway Vincent, Cameron, Bunny, and this guy named Milton were sitting on Bunny's stoop when some guys drove up and started calling Cameron names. Cameron told them to kiss his ass, and one of the guys pulled a piece and started shooting. Everybody jumped off the stoop and started running.

The only one who got hit was Vincent, and at first it didn't seem so bad. He was walking around with a bullet hole in his side. He said he couldn't walk too good and they put him on Cameron's bike and took him to the hospital. He went in the emergency room and had to wait like an hour and a half because the nurse who looked at him said it didn't seem too bad. When he got in and they x-rayed him he was feeling worse. At first they said the bullet just missed something vital and he was lucky. But the next morning he couldn't walk at all. That's what's going down with him now. He can't walk at all. That is just right on sad because everybody wants to walk.

Things are going okay. I tried to transfer

to Frederick Douglass Academy but they didn't have any room at FDA. If I went to FDA I could walk to school every day. Also, there aren't as many fights up there.

Yo, Reese, I'll be glad when you get out because there isn't anyone to hang out with anymore. Everybody is either into a hustle or doing crimes. I'm trying to keep straight like you said, but I really need somebody to hang with who isn't being shot at or drugging up or getting into trouble.

My moms said if I got a college scholarship it would be good. I'd like to go away to school, maybe one of those big schools with a football team that plays on television and a million cheerleaders with fat legs (smile).

I saw your brother Willis the other day. He was sitting on the rail in front of your building. He looked like he didn't have nothing to do, the same as everybody else. Yo, Reese, when you get out we should maybe work for a year and then buy a car. We could have a gypsy cab business. I could drive it in the day and you could drive at night and once in a while we would switch up. Unless I got a scholarship. I'm not *too hopeful about the scholarship anymore.*

Anyway, take care of yourself and come home soon.

Kenneth Bramble

K-Man was smart enough to get a scholarship and he didn't play ball or anything like that. Most of the white guys that got scholarships did a lot of extracurricular stuff. One white guy I knew even went to Africa and climbed Mount Kilimanjaro with his grandfather. I wish I had done that. My mom's father had a stroke when he was thirty and could hardly walk. I never saw my father's father. My father never talked about him either.

The fight between King Kong Tarik and Toon was supposed to take place after supper. I watched Toon looking down at his tray and knew he was thinking about being beaten up again. Diego, that punk, was sitting with King Kong, making jokes and nudging him and stuff, and every once in a while he would look over at Toon.

There was always some little guy around for people like Tarik to beat on. It was like they spent all their lives looking for victims, somebody they could make feel bad.

Mr. Pugh was on the rec room detail but he always took long breaks because he was sneaking smokes. Diego and Leon were sitting next to Toon, and when Mr. Pugh got up to go to the bathroom, they pulled him out of his chair and pushed him toward King Kong.

King Kong knew Toon wouldn't fight back and started goofing on him, faking punches and winding up and stuff.

"Mr. Pugh is going to come back soon," Diego said. He was standing at the door looking through the window down the corridor toward the staff men's room.

When he said that, King Kong threw a hard punch and hit Toon on the top of his shoulder and the side of his head. Toon went down on one knee, and then King Kong started punching him in the back of his head.

Toon whimpered and put up one hand to block the blows.

"Put your hand down!" King Kong stood over Toon, ready to hit him again.

Toon lowered his hand and King Kong punched him on the back of his neck.

"Oh, man, that hurt!" Leon said.

Toon was down on his hands and knees.

"He putting his butt up for you to kick!" Diego said.

King Kong started backing up to get a running start. He backed all the way up against the couch and started toward Toon. That's when I tripped him.

King Kong stumbled, caught himself, and spun around. I clipped him upside his jaw. He was surprised and his hands went out to his sides like he was trying to steady himself. I jabbed him with my left hand and turned my fist sideways and hit him in the side of his face with everything I had.

"Here comes Mr. Pugh!" Diego called out.

I looked at King Kong, and he was down on the ground lying on his side. Play grabbed Toon and pulled him up and pushed him into a chair. Diego got back to a chair, but King Kong was still lying down when Mr. Pugh opened the door.

"What the hell's going on?" he asked, looking around the room. "I said, 'What the hell's going on?'"

Mr. Pugh went over to where King Kong was lying and turned his head from side to side. "You been cut?" he asked.

"He hit me!" He was on one elbow pointing at me.

"Ain't nobody hit him," Play said. "Clumsy sucker just fell."

Mr. Pugh wasn't buying it. He grabbed me and spun me around with one hand behind my back. He cuffed me and then dragged me out of the rec room and down the hall to the detention room.

"You trying to get me into trouble, you little punk?" He had his mouth just about on my ear as he unlocked the detention room door.

He didn't have to cuff me to the wall restraint, but he did. Then he put one fat hand around my neck and started squeezing.

"Leave a bruise, man," I said. "Leave a bruise!"

He lowered his hand and then threw his shoulder into me, bouncing me into the wall. I looked into his face. It was twisted and mad.

He said something I couldn't understand, spitting all over me as he talked. Then he left.

A minute later, I heard King Kong coming down the hall. He was yelling he didn't do nothing, and I knew Mr. Pugh had his ass headed for the other detention room. Even from where I was I could hear the bumps against the wall.

"Hit him one for me!" I called out.

CHAPTER 20

Mr. Pugh and Mr. Wilson brought King Kong, Toon, and me into the large intake room and cuffed us to wall rings behind the long bench. We were about three feet from each other with me on one end of the bench, King Kong on the other, and Toon in the middle. Mr. Pugh walked over to the door, turned, and gave us the finger before he left, slamming the door behind him.

"I wish I could reach your black butt," King Kong said. "I'd tear your damned head off."

"If you can sing it, you can bring it," I said. "I ain't going nowhere. You'll get your chance. Then we'll see what happens."

"You won't be able to sucker-punch me next

time, faggot," King Kong said.

Then *Toon* turned and spit at King Kong, which surprised me because I knew King Kong was just looking for a reason to beat Toon silly.

But I liked that. Toon couldn't fight and he was little and kind of punkish, but he still made a statement.

King Kong started telling Toon what he was going to do to him, how he was going to shotgun him and make him call him uncle and a whole bunch of other crap. Toon looked up in the air and shook his head like he wasn't hearing him.

Mr. Cintron came in with Mr. Pugh a moment later and told Pugh to uncuff Toon.

"Mr. Deepak, you are scheduled for one day in detention quarters and one week's loss of privileges," he said.

Mr. Pugh took Toon out of the room. All the while Mr. Cintron was looking at some papers he had in front of him. I thought he was going to come down on me the hardest. He didn't say anything until Mr. Pugh came back and he motioned for him to uncuff King Kong.

"Mr. Sanders, you are scheduled for five days in

detention quarters and one week's loss of privileges," Mr. Cintron said.

Mr. Pugh took King Kong out but not before that stupid jerk could give me another dirty look.

"Reese, when you're standing up, perhaps reaching for something in your closet, and you sit down suddenly, do you get headaches?" Mr. Cintron asked.

"No, sir," I said. "I never get headaches."

"Well, that's kind of funny because your brains are up your ass," he said. "Aren't they?"

"No, sir."

"What do you want to call this institution?"

"You mean Progress?" I asked.

"Yes."

Mr. Pugh walked back into the room and came over to where we were.

"A juvenile correctional facility, I guess."

"James, you ever see a basket of crabs?" Mr. Cintron turned to Mr. Pugh.

"Yeah, I've seen them," Mr. Pugh said, smiling.

"What happens when one of the crabs tries to get out?" Mr. Cintron asked.

"The other crabs pull him back in," Mr. Pugh said. "No way one of them is getting out unless the rest of them are half dead."

"Ninety percent of the inmates here aren't going anywhere with their lives and they know it. It's not because they can't, it's because they simply won't. They know it, and every time they see somebody who looks like he might break the cycle and do something with his life, they want to pull him back in," Mr. Cintron said. "Especially if you look like them, if you come from the same environment they come from. If you turn your life around, you're putting the blame on them for not turning theirs around. Sanders will take another year on his time before he'd let you alone. You don't get it, right?"

"I get it now," I said.

"No, you don't get it," Mr. Cintron said. "You know it, but you don't know it well enough to control yourself. You have five days in detention and one week's loss of privileges. Take him out of here."

The detention cell is a little smaller than the rest of the cells and just about bare. There's a small window near the ceiling, but it's too high to see out of. If you run across the floor and jump up, you can see the sky, but that's about it. The toilet is fourteen inches high, which means you have to squat down to use it. There is a water fountain, with a button on top. When you push the button, the water comes up from a small hole in the middle of the fountain. The water is warm. It comes up about an inch out of the hole, so you have to put your mouth almost on top of it to get a drink. Nothing in the room sticks out more than a quarter of an inch except the door-knob, and that is tapered so you can't hook anything onto it. That way you can't make a noose out of a strip of cloth or a shoelace. In the detention cell, you can't kill yourself.

There is writing on the wall across from the bed—messages from other guys or girls who have been in the room. One says: "Time lost can never be found again." Another one says: "I hate myself." Above it, someone has written, "I hate you, too," and drawn an arrow pointing to the sign that says, "I hate myself."

Each time I think there is no place lower to go, I find that there is at least one place that will mess you up worse than you were. And there were signs that made you remember if you forgot. When I lay on the cot in the detention cell and looked at the doorknob, I knew that whoever designed the room knew I would think about killing myself. No, they were saying, we understand how you're feeling but you can't do that, either.

In the detention cell, you get fed before the others. You have to stand against the far wall with your back toward the door. Then they open the door and put your tray on the floor. When my supper came, I felt like turning around and yelling, "Boo!" But I knew that would just get me more time.

Lights-out in detention was at 8:30, same as it was with levels three, four, and five.

The first day lasted two hundred hours. Then the days really got long.

"You got five days in detention," they'd said. No, all my life I was going to be in detention. All my life I was going to be locked down in some cell or in some life with steel bars, keeping me from getting up and going someplace or dying and not feeling bad anymore.

I thought about K-Man's letter. I didn't care about Vincent being shot because I didn't know him. In my life, somebody was always being shot or being beat up or being killed. I was somebody you needed to stay away from, someone who might hurt you or get you killed. Someone I wasn't recognizing anymore.

The second day in detention. I was thinking of fighting King Kong. I wondered if he was in his cell doing push-ups and maybe some squats to keep in shape. I got up and did some push-ups but my heart wasn't in it. If King Kong attacked me I would just have to go all out and wreck the dude. Maybe they would send me upstate and I would have to be with grown men who could beat me up whenever they wanted to do it. Maybe if I found somebody up there who was cool, I could get a shank and stab whoever messed with me. That's what they did upstate. You had to let them know you would stab them to death or they would take advantage of you. A little guy like Toon would just be somebody's woman unless he found a way to kill himself.

My father had been in jail. He wasn't tough. Not inside. Outside he could beat me when I was little, or Willis before he got good with his hands, but he wasn't tough. He did a lot of cursing and throwing himself around when he was drinking, but it wouldn't be long before I could take him one on one. Although, really, it's tough to kick your father's ass because that's a little like kicking your own ass. Maybe him hitting me or Willis was like him hitting himself. I don't know.

Me, Toon, and King Kong was all in a place under the real world. If they let us loose after breakfast—just let us walk out the front door—we wouldn't have no place to go. Toon would go back to his parents so they could yell at him and go back to being small and pushed around. King Kong, he would go back to swinging on trees and climbing up buildings and being stupid, because sometimes settling for stupid was easier than reaching for anything better. If you gave him a free bus pass, he couldn't get nowhere because there wasn't anyplace for him to get to. He would just be riding around in a circle until he got to the same place he started from.

Me, I would go home, and everybody would look at me and ask me what I wanted.

"What you want?"

"I don't know," I would answer. "What you got?"

"Don't worry about it because you ain't getting what I got," they would say. "And I'm watching you too."

That was the truth. My father didn't have nothing. Willis didn't have nothing. Mom was just checking out the world to see what she could snatch off. The hurting part was that if you checked everything out, peeped what was going down, everybody knew the same thing. They knew that me and Toon and King Kong didn't have no place to go in this world and maybe we would try to slip out to dying when they wasn't looking. They knew that, so they put us in these cells where you couldn't even kill yourself.

CHAPTER 22

Another morning, another cold breakfast. I dreamed about Toon. In my dream he was in the visiting room and his parents were sitting there shaking their heads and sucking their teeth and looking at each other like they were so ashamed of Toon. If they really ever got into Toon's head, they would never find their way out. They would be lost for freaking ever and be scared out of their minds because they would know what the real world looked like.

Sometimes, when I see Toon, I think he looks like how I would look if I could see inside myself. Little and stupid looking and scared, knowing I was going to get beat up every day. When I think about Toon, I want to cry. I'm glad I'm in detention. In detention you are all by yourself and nobody can see how bad you feel. Sometimes I think that people in the outside world know how bad you feel. They know it, but then they pass it off by just giving you a label, like *criminal* or *felon.*

If you're out in the world feeling bad enough to take dope to lighten it up a little, or if you're so mad at the world you're ready to break somebody up or chalk them out, then they just switch your ass from who you think you are to what they got on your rap sheet, and they don't have to feel sorry for you no more because you're not human.

Another day went by, maybe two. It didn't matter.

One day there was a shadow on the floor. I thought it might have been a bird in the window. I got up quick and looked, but it was gone. A shadow that might have been a bird.

When Mr. Pugh banged on my door, I jumped. I got up and went across the room and put my chest against the wall and my hands behind my back like I was supposed to.

"Mr. Pugh, what meal is this?"

"Shut up!"

"How many days have I been in here?"

"Shut up!"

The door slammed and I turned around and went to the tray. A container of apple juice, string beans, corn, chicken wings, applesauce, bread, and a cup of ice cream. I ate it. Then I sat down on the floor and watched as the room grew darker. The light from the rectangular window made an image on the floor that went halfway across and just touched the opposite wall.

Later, Mr. Cintron came to the door.

"Next week you go back to Evergreen," he said through the grating. "It's not for you, because you don't deserve it. I'm letting you go back because I want the program to at least look like it's working."

I didn't answer him.

"Anderson! You all right in there?"

"I'm all right," I said.

I can do this.

I thought of school and what the teacher had said about sundials. All you needed was a fixed object and a shadow and you could figure out the time. But where did the first time come from? I didn't have any markers or I could have made marks on the floor and then figured the time as the sun moved through the window. The window was the fixed object and the shadow was wherever the light wasn't shining. The first thing I had to do was to cop the time from whoever brought me a meal. Then I would mark that off, and the next time they brought me a meal I would mark that off, and then divide that into sections.

The room was getting darker. Soon it would be so dark I would have to feel my way to the cot. But I wasn't feeling bad about it anymore. Maybe if I stayed in detention for months, or even years, it would be different. But I could put up with bad stuff happening to me.

Then why do I fight all the time?

Because fighting is good. When you fight you're alive, you're somebody. You're not standing in the corridor with your hands behind your back. Maybe that's it, that you're free, swinging your fists, letting people know who you are. Even if you're going to die. That kid who beat up Mr. Hooft, maybe he knew more than Mr. Hooft thought. Maybe he knew he was going to die but needed to be somebody for that minute. Like the guys in the hood running down the streets throwing signs and spitting smack like they're bulletproof but knowing they aren't. Knowing they aren't.

I could do detention. Sitting there in the dark, trembling as the minutes slipped by. It didn't make any difference how slow it went. I was locked in and the rest of the world was locked out. I couldn't touch them, but they couldn't touch me, either.

I'm all right.

When they finally let me out, I was jumpy, off balance. It's how they wanted me to feel.

CHAPTER 23

"Where's your beard, man?"

"What beard?"

"In the movies when a guy gets out of the hole, he comes stumbling out and he's got a beard and everything," Play said. "You supposed to be squinting and staggering around."

"It was kind of hard," I said.

"It was hard out here, too," Play said. "Since they had you in detention, we were getting steak every day to see how we liked it. Steak with mashed potatoes and gravy. Man, you know how boring that gets?"

"Get out of here, Play," I said. "You guys weren't getting no steak. If they gave you steak, you wouldn't leave when your date came up. You'd be hanging around for the eats."

"I decided what I'm going to do when I get out of here," Play said.

"What?"

"I'm going to be a rich white dude," he said. "Then I won't have to do nothing but sit around and worry about people like you coming into my neighborhood."

"Yeah, well, I decided what I'm going to do too," I said. "I'm going to look around for a rich white dude like you and take his stuff."

It was good talking to Play again. It was good just talking. I could see guys going crazy being locked up for years like they did in the max prisons where you were on lockdown twenty-three hours a day. In a way I didn't seem to be alive when I was in detention. Being alive wasn't about just breathing and whatnot. It was like you could look around and somebody else would notice that you were alive. Talking helped a lot, because when somebody answered, it meant they heard you. Even if somebody was yelling at you, it was better than silence. I knew if I was in lockdown long enough, I would probably talk to myself.

On my first day back from detention, I sat with Play at breakfast and listened to him complain about the eggs. I wanted to say something about the eggs being different when you ate them in the dining room, but I couldn't find the words that made it sound right. Eggs are eggs, and they shouldn't taste different if you ate them in one room or the other. But they did.

King Kong looked over at me from the corner of the room, and it made me laugh because he was still trying to look hard even though I had put him down good.

I didn't say nothing in school, even though I wanted to. When we left class for lunch, King Kong came real near me and brushed me a little. I gave him a look and he stopped and turned toward me, and Mr. Pugh came over and pushed us both against the wall.

"Cool it, girls!"

I knew Play was in because he cut a dude on Clinton Avenue in Brooklyn. King Kong wasn't keeping his square ass together after a beat down and I was wondering if I would have to shank him to get him off my case.

"Yo, Play, how it feel to cut a guy?" I asked.

"I don't know," he said. "I was just swinging and it happened. I won the blade playing Horse. I hit five shots in a row and I got the guy's blade, which wasn't no big deal because he had a whole trunkful of them."

My first afternoon out of detention was cool. Group was canceled because Miss Dodson's car had broken down on the highway and she couldn't make it. We went right to recreation and personal hygiene, and I checked myself out for a beard. Nothing.

Toon came over and sat with me in the rec room. He handed me a book.

"It's a gift," he said. "From me to you."

The book was *Lord of the Flies.*

"You don't have to give me a gift," I said.

Toon shrugged and looked down at the floor. "It's because in my heart we are brothers," he said. "I had a brother. In our family, he was the hero. My father said his name should have been Rama, but he wanted him to have an American name so he named him Raymond. When my brother Raymond was alive, he was the center of my family. He was smart and tall and looked very handsome. When he became sick and died, my family was very hurt.

"They took his ashes to India and scattered them in a river near where our family had lived before my grandfather came to America. I was very excited to go to India for the first time, but my father was mad at me for thinking about what I would see there instead of mourning for my brother. After that, he hardly ever spoke to me."

"What was India like?" I asked.

"Like the Bronx, but with more animals and older buses," Toon said.

"Your brother got shot?"

"No, he had a cough and his chest hurt, but my father said it was nothing. Even when he coughed a lot, my father said it was just making him stronger. Then he had to go to the hospital, and after two days, he died."

"I'm sorry about that," I said. "But you don't have to give me your book."

"You don't want to be my brother," Toon said. "But in my heart, you are."

"Okay, you're my brother too," I said.

Toon smiled and then went back over to where he had been sitting.

Toon was okay. He wasn't like a real brother. He wasn't like a real friend like K-Man or even Play. He was little and weak and goofy looking, the kind of kid anybody could mess with. In a way I wanted him to be okay all the time, but in another way I felt bad about him, as if it was something bad about him that made him weak. Even though I could get busy with my hands and could deal if I had to, there was also something in me that could be hurt like Toon. Not hurt, maybe. Not even bruised or nothing. Just fucked with.

I took the book back to my room after rec time. I didn't know if I was going to read it or not.

Sometimes, when things get stupid, I just shut it all out and, like, start all over again. So when I woke up in the morning in my own room, I was feeling good and thinking good stuff. Usually when I woke up, it was five thirty or five forty-five, before the rooms were unlocked, which was exactly six. I must have been tired, because I woke up just as the bell rang and I got up real quick, cleaned the room for inspection, and got dressed.

Mr. Pugh took us to breakfast, and Diego asked him what we were having.

"Eggs, sausages, hash browns, and juice," he said. "Real eggs today, not that crap that comes in a box. They're buying them from local merchants now, so we blend in with the community."

"We could go out and rob a local bank," Play said, "and then spend it on some local girls."

"Shut up!" Mr. Pugh said. He was smiling.

Mr. Pugh was right. We did have real eggs instead of those scrambled eggs.

"How you want your eggs?" the fat round cook asked me. Griffin could make the eggs either hard or almost hard. He wouldn't make them over easy no matter what you said.

"Poached," I said. "With some caviar on the side."

He broke two eggs and dropped them on the grill, and I watched as they got done on one side before he flipped them and cooked them hard on the other. No big deal.

Toon sat by himself two tables down from me and Play, and I was wondering if I should ask him to come over to where we were sitting when Mr. Wilson entered. He looked around and called over to me.

"Anderson, let's go," he said.

"Where I'm going?"

"Get your ass up out of the seat," he said, "and let's go."

I didn't like Mr. Wilson's tone and figured something was going on. When he took me out in the hallway, King Kong pointed at me and started laughing. I figured that ugly sucker must have told some lies on me.

We got to the administrative wing and he unlocked the doors and my heart went cold.

"Yo, man, they sending me upstate?"

Mr. Wilson was a cool guy, but he didn't answer me and I figured I was gone. Nobody had said anything about me going upstate, but I knew I had had two fights. I thought about Cobo, the guy I had fought when he first came to Progress. They had sent him upstate, but he was headed there in the first place.

"You need to pee?" Mr. Wilson asked me. We were standing in front of the bathroom.

I went in but I couldn't pee. I felt like I had to but I was too uptight so I came out.

"Wash your damned hands," Mr. Wilson said.

I went back in and washed my hands. When I returned, Mr. Wilson took his cuffs and made a spinning motion with his index finger.

No matter how bad you feel when you're locked up, you feel worse when you get cuffed. It's like you ain't human or something. You're some kind of *thing* that needs to be restrained.

Mr. Wilson took me to the office and signed me out. The clerk, a little fat lady, was looking at me and I felt naked.

"I can't take none of my stuff with me?" I asked.

Mr. Wilson took me by the arm and started walking me through the wing toward the side door. We went into the yard and it was a nice day. Sunny, bright, with birds walking around on the grass.

The back of the transportation van has rings on the sides and I was cuffed to one of them. We drove for almost two hours. I could tell because Mr. Wilson was listening to the news on the radio the whole time. From where I was sitting, I couldn't see out the back window but I could see through the front window when Mr. Wilson moved his head a little. I could tell we were in a city and I could see black people. I thought that maybe something had happened at home, somebody had died or something, and they were taking me to the funeral. I figured it had to be either Mom or Willis. They wouldn't take me to see my father because he didn't live with me, and I couldn't imagine anything happening to Icy. I didn't think God liked me, but I didn't think He would let Icy get hurt.

When the van stopped and Mr. Wilson came to take me out, I saw a small crowd of Puerto Rican–looking people on the sidewalk. I wondered if they were waiting for me. Mr. Wilson got me to the sidewalk, locked the van, and then started making a call on his cell. I looked around and recognized where I was. I was in front of the 135th Street precinct and I figured I had been right—that something had happened in my family. Mr. Wilson finished his call and then took me into the precinct.

He led me to the sergeant at the desk and gave him my name and number from Progress. Another cop came and got me, and he and Mr. Wilson went with me up a flight of stairs and put me in a small room. It was about the size of the detention room at Progress. The room looked hard. There was a table with three chairs, two on one side and one on the other. The cop pointed toward the one chair.

"Sit there," he said.

I sat down, still cuffed, and the cop and Mr.

Wilson left. I didn't hear them lock the door, but I saw there wasn't a doorknob on the inside of it.

The room was painted dark on the bottom, a reddish brown, and green on top. There weren't any windows or nothing. In a corner I saw a camera and there was a red indicator light next to it. I knew somebody could look at me through the camera and maybe even tape me.

For a while, I tried to look cool, like I was innocent or something and then that made me laugh. How you supposed to look when you innocent? I told myself if I ever got back to Progress, I was going to tell Play about how I was trying to look.

When you in a room with no clock and nobody there to talk to, you can't tell how long you been in it. It seemed like a long time, and I was beginning to feel like I had to go to the bathroom. I knew they wanted to make me feel uncomfortable. Being in a chair and handcuffed was uncomfortable all by itself. I stretched my legs out and tried to relax.

This wasn't nothing about somebody being hurt or anything. This was about something else. I wasn't worried about it because the only thing I ever did I got caught for and was up in Progress ever since.

I thought maybe Willis did something and they wanted to know what I knew about it. If I did know something I wasn't going to snitch, but I didn't know anything. That was the truth whether they believed it or not.

I was glad for the camera. At least they couldn't beat me up. Or maybe they could. Just turn the camera off a little while and kick my ass, then turn it back on.

When the door opened, I jumped. Two guys, one white and one black, came in. The black guy was real big, about six feet two or six feet three, and dark skinned. He had a cigar in his mouth. He took it out and looked at it like he was real interested in it and then he took his jacket off. He had a holster on but he didn't have a gun in it. The white guy was wearing a soft shirt and was big but a little fat. He put a folder on the desk.

"We thought you were light stuff," the black guy said. "What you think about that?"

"I don't know what you talking about," I said. Up at Progress they always said to never talk to the police or answer any questions no matter what happened because they will just hang your butt. I didn't want to talk or answer any questions.

"This is Detective Browning and I'm John Rhodes, Mr. Anderson," the white guy said. "You don't have to remember our names."

"You need water or anything?" the black guy said. "You hungry?"

"I just had breakfast," I said.

"Before we ask you any questions, we have to read you your rights," the white guy said. "Just listen to them. 'You have the right to remain silent and refuse to answer questions. Anything you say may be used against you in a court of law. You have the right to consult an attorney before speaking to the police and to have an attorney present during questioning now or in the future. If you cannot afford an attorney, if you wish, one will be appointed for you before any questioning. If you decide to answer questions now without an attorney present, you will still have the right to stop answering at any time until you talk to an attorney. Knowing and understanding your rights as I have explained them to you, are you willing to answer my questions without an attorney present?'"

"I don't want to answer any questions," I said.

"Fine, no problem," the white detective said. "But

did you understand the rights?"

"Yeah."

"And you know you're facing twenty years?"

"For what? I've been up in Progress for almost two years, so I couldn't have done anything."

"You were arrested for stealing and distributing prescription pads, right?" the black detective asked.

"Yeah."

"You hooked up with Freddy Booker?"

"Yeah."

"Booker said that you also stole some drugs, which you cut and distributed," the black guy went on. "Is that right?"

"No, man."

"Well, he's swearing to it, and some of the drugs that were involved have caused the death of an addict," the white detective said.

"He said I did that two years ago?"

"I think he's lying," the black detective said. "He's lying to save his ass."

"He's in jail, right?" I said.

"No, he's on parole," the white detective said. "He got some time off for cooperating in another case. But he got busted for distribution, and he said he got the drugs from you."

"Two years ago?"

"He said you stashed them with your brother—"

"Willis." The white detective opened up the folder. "Your brother is Willis Anderson?"

"Yeah, but—"

"Does he use drugs?"

"No," I said.

"So if he's got a stash, he must be selling the shit, right?"

"I don't know what you talking about," I said. "And I don't want to answer any more questions."

"This is what I was talking to you about," the black detective said to the white guy. "He wants to lawyer up because he knows the deal."

"There ain't no deal," I said. "And I don't want to answer any more questions."

"You know, Billy"— the white guy turned to the black detective—"you think Anderson here is willing to take the twenty years because he's looking to beat a murder-one rap? I mean, it makes sense. With the twenty, he gets out in sixteen max; maybe he can manage an appeal or something and get out in ten. If they give him the full bid on murder one, he can get life without the possibility of parole. You think he's just playing it smart?"

"I don't know why he's taking the twenty to cover for Booker, though," the black guy said. Then he turned to me. "You and Booker real tight?"

"I don't even know the sucker," I said. "I just peeped his play around the neighborhood, that's all."

"Look, he doesn't want to tell us if Booker was dealing drugs even if we can offer him a plea," the white guy said. "We can offer him five and he'd be on the street in three. He's got something to hide so he's keeping mum. Isn't that right?"

"Let's not deal with him," the black detective said. "He'd rather do the twenty calendars than talk to us. That's the way these people are."

"Okay, send him back to jail," the white guy said. "We know where to find him, and when the trial comes up, we'll tell them that he don't want no deal. He wants the full twenty. How's your daughter? Did she get to watch the game the other night?" They were headed toward the door.

"No, her mom made her do her homework, but I taped it for her," the black guy said as he was leaving the room.

When I watched television, it never seemed real, because on television, people solved all their problems in, like, thirty minutes. The only thing that was going on in my life was whether the garbage was bad enough that I didn't mind people seeing me cry.

I got to Progress and was put in detention because everybody was too busy to take me to group.

"Two years? They reaching all the way back two years?" Play asked me at supper.

"I told that to Wilson on the drive up here," I said. "At first he didn't say nothing, but then he said it was either about a homicide or they're just fishing."

"Fishing for what?"

"How I know? I haven't heard anything from the guys on the block. I haven't heard anything from the attorney who handled my case. I haven't heard anything from anybody!"

"So who did you sell the pads to?" Play asked.

"I don't even remember the dude's name," I said. That was a lie, but I remembered an old gangster used to sit on the stoop all the time saying you should never discuss your case with anybody in jail because they could be a snitch.

"I can't figure it," Play was saying.

I could figure it some. What I saw was people walking around and anytime they got some crap on their shoes, they needed to wipe it off. Somehow me and Play and Toon and even King Kong wasn't nothing but the crap on their shoes.

After supper, Mr. Cintron pulled me aside and told me he still had faith in me. I didn't believe him. I had messed up too many times. I knew the deal was that he wanted the work program to work. I could dig that. It would have been better if they had taken Play for the program or even Toon. I guessed that Toon was too young, and Play was at Progress for a violent crime.

I didn't go to Evergreen for three days because

of an administrative inspection that was coming up. They were long days and I could feel myself getting depressed. It was like a dark cloud was creeping over me and I couldn't do anything about it.

When I got to Evergreen, I was feeling a little better because at least time went faster when I was busy. Mr. Hooft was sitting in a chair in the corner waiting for me.

"It wasn't you, was it?" He was kind of half shouting at me, and his voice, which wasn't too strong from jump street, cracked when he spoke.

"What wasn't me?" I asked.

"Somebody messed my bed up!" he said, jabbing a finger in the direction of his bed. "You going to clean it?"

"Yeah."

Somebody had moved their bowels in his bed, and I had an idea of who it was. I took the sheet and folded it up quick, pulled the pillow out of the pillow case and put the stinky sheet inside, and headed for the laundry room. Simi was in the hallway.

"What are you doing?" she asked.

"Mr. Hooft's bed got messed up," I said.

"Usually he blames me for it," she said, taking the bundle from me. "Get some clean linen from the nurse at the station desk. And don't forget to see if his pad is wet."

"I was wondering if it was you," I said.

She hit me lightly on the back of the head.

I got clean linen, returned to Mr. Hooft's room, and checked the pad in the middle of the bed. It was dry, but I turned it over anyway.

"They let anybody walk into this place," he said.

"You been outside today?" I asked. "The weather is real nice."

"They don't let me go outside," he answered. "They think I'm going to get a bus and go to California."

"You ever been to California?"

Before he could answer, a guy came into the room. I thought he was a doctor because he was wearing a suit. He didn't say nothing but just stood in the doorway and pointed at me.

"This is Reese," Mr. Hooft said. "He's a criminal. He killed maybe three or four people—I don't know—he won't tell me how many. They let him come to keep the old people in line."

"I'm John Hooft," the man said. "If anything

is missing from my grandfather's room, I'll get it back."

"Nothing missing from here," I said. "I just come over—"

"I don't have any time today, Grandpa," the man said, putting his hands in his pockets. "I have to get over to the dealership and straighten some people out. Clara called. She wants to know if you got the check she sent."

"They told me they received a check," Mr. Hooft said quietly.

"Okay, it was for twenty-five dollars, and I'll ask at the office when I come back next week to make sure that every penny of it is spent on you."

"Okay, John." Mr. Hooft nodded as he spoke. His voice seemed to be getting weaker.

John turned and looked me up and down, like he was measuring me. I had seen the look a hundred times, guys thinking they can kick your ass and letting you know it. Then he turned back to Mr. Hooft.

"So I'll tell Clara that everything is fine?"

"Everything is fine," Mr. Hooft said. "Sure. How are her children?"

"I guess they're okay," John said. "She's always whining about them. If she calls you, tell her I came to see you. And if you have any problems, tell her and she can tell me. You understand that?"

"Yes, sure," Mr. Hooft said.

John went over and put his face near his grandfather and gave him a half of a kiss on the cheek. Then he turned on one heel and walked out of the room.

"Busy man," Mr. Hooft said after he was gone. "He's got two minutes to spare on a sunny day, one minute if there's a cloud in the sky."

"He acts like a tough guy," I said.

"Tough? What does he know about being tough? What do you know about being tough?" Mr. Hooft asked. "Does swinging your fist make you tough? Does hitting a man make you tough? Do you think you would hit—what's his name? That little Negro who looks like a bull—Mike Tyson? Would you hit him? Would you?"

"No."

"Because he would kill you! Am I right?"

"Yeah."

"Well, sonny, Reese—which is no name for a boy,

but your people make up names—you should try being old. Because old is tough and you don't swing at being old because old always kills you. So what do you think of that?"

"Well . . ."

"He's going to go home and call everybody and say . . . and say that he came and he visited me even though . . . even though he didn't have a lot of time. . . ." Mr. Hooft was crying.

"Yo, man, you need some water or something?" I asked.

"In five years, maybe I've had three visits, maybe four visits," he said. "They celebrate their heritage. They go back to the Netherlands and they weren't born there. They are no more Dutch than you are. But they can't come to see me and I was born there."

Mr. Hooft's eyes seemed different. They were darker when he cried, almost like a bird's eyes. I wanted to go over and put my arm around him or something, but I didn't. I did think about beating up his grandson. He was looking me up and down, but I wondered how he would have felt if I had landed some thunder upside his head.

"Don't sit on my bed," Mr. Hooft spoke softly.

"Excuse me?"

"Don't sit on my bed," he said. "That's how it gets messed up."

I cleaned his room real good. Before I left, I let him put his arm around my shoulder so he could get up on the bed. He was wearing a hospital gown and I could see his legs. They were thin and white and wrinkly.

I got the top of the bed up a little for him and started to bring the bottom up too, but he wanted his legs straight.

"Sometimes they cramp up if I have them bent," he said. "Then I have to straighten them out really slow."

I sat in the corner thinking about his grandson. I thought that maybe Mr. Hooft didn't have a lot of interesting things to say to him.

"You know, I don't get many visits, either," I said.

"Well, you have to remember"—Mr. Hooft was smiling—"you're not too good-looking."

"When you . . . when you were in that children's camp," I asked him, "did you ever think about just starting a fight with one of the guards and, you know, getting it over with?"

Mr. Hooft turned to me, looked in my face for a long moment, and then turned toward the window. "We lived nine to a hut," he said. "There was never enough to eat, never enough hope to spread around to nine boys. Sometimes I wished it would just end. But I didn't want to be shot or die by violence. I didn't have that kind of courage. But then one day I saw, behind the huts, in a corner, some flowers. Jasmine. You know jasmine?"

"No."

"Beautiful flower. It was closed tight during the day, but at night it opened up and somehow I thought that flower was like me. Afraid to speak when I was around the guards, always scared that I would do something wrong and they would hurt me. But at night I would lie on my cot, and I would dream about other things. About our home in Java, about my mother. And when I took my mind away from how miserable I felt, things became better for me. I would be out in the fields digging a ditch or piling up rocks around the wells—the Japanese had us doing that a lot—but I would think about that flower and I would worry about it and be anxious for it to be all right when I returned to the hut. It wasn't much, but it was better than stewing in my own juices."

All the time he was talking to me he was looking out of the window. From where he was, I knew, he couldn't see much. The sky was gray and there were clouds in the distance. After a while, I could see that he had fallen asleep. I stayed in the corner. Simi brought me some magazines to read and I leafed through them until it was time to go.

On the way back to Progress, I kept thinking of Mr. Hooft as a kid digging a ditch with a guard watching him. I could imagine how scared he was. I was feeling sorry for him being scared back then, even if it had happened a long time ago.

Mr. Hooft's life was harder than I had thought it was. All the time he was talking about how much he had done in his life, it was all a front. A lot of people seemed to be making up their lives, and I guessed if you didn't have anything else really going on, it was the thing to do. But it was sad.

Mr. Cintron called me to the office and pointed toward a chair. He took a sip of his coffee, made a little face, and then leaned back in his chair.

"You hear there was a fight in the corridor yesterday afternoon?" he asked.

"Nobody told me," I said. I was surprised, because usually Play clues me in on all the happenings.

"Diego punched Leon Muñoz in the back of the head," Mr. Cintron said.

"And Leon is supposed to be his boy, too," I said. "Diego is just foul."

"So how does that make you feel?"

"How does it make me feel? I feel like it's just wrong, that's all," I said.

"You want some coffee?"

"I should take some," I said. "But I don't like it."

"You want to talk about what happened at the precinct yesterday?" he asked.

"Nothing happened," I said. "They said they were considering laying some new charges on me and I didn't know what they were talking about. You know, I got busted two years ago for taking some prescription pads and—"

"*Stealing* some prescription pads—"

"Yeah, stealing some prescription pads," I said. "Now they're saying somebody took some drugs from the doctor's office, too. I didn't do that and I've never heard of anybody laying on charges for something that happened two years ago and it wasn't homicide."

"The detectives called me after you left and said that you were considering copping a plea," Mr. Cintron said. "They said you were facing twenty years and you were looking to cop to a lesser for three years."

"They might have said that, but I still don't know what they're talking about. They said that Little Freddy told them that I took the drugs from the doctor's office and messed with them, and then I sold them and somebody died—"

"That's homicide. 'Somebody died' is automatically homicide until it gets to the D.A.'s office and he makes the final decision about what the charge is going to be."

"But I didn't take any drugs out of the doctor's office. I took the pads. The prescription pads were all I took. He had some money on the desk and I didn't even take that."

"Why not?"

"Because I was scared and wanted to get out of there. I know some guys get off breaking into people's houses and offices and things, but I don't," I said. "Soon as I was inside his office, I was looking to snatch some pads and run."

"You knew where the pads were?"

"Yeah, Freddy told me."

"What's Freddy been doing this last year or so?" Mr. Cintron was putting more sugar in his coffee. "If I gave you the phone, could you find out what he was doing?"

"I don't know. I could ask my brother or maybe my friend, but I don't want to get them involved in nothing."

"If you're not involved in anything, and if you

didn't take the drugs like the city detectives are saying, how can you get somebody else involved?" Mr. Cintron asked.

"Yo, I don't mean any disrespect, sir, but how am I involved?" I asked. "Y'all took me down there and they questioned me and told me about the drugs and I didn't know anything about them."

Mr. Cintron pushed the phone toward me. "Call your brother," he said.

"I don't know if I should," I said.

"It's unofficial, just between you and me," Mr. Cintron said.

I picked up the phone and dialed home. I was hoping that Mom or Icy answered.

"The Andersons!" Icy.

"Hey, baby girl, how you doing?"

"Reese, how you doing?" she asked. "You coming home?"

"No, not yet," I said. "Say, Icy, is Willis home?"

"You don't want to talk to me?"

"I do, but this is about some business," I said. "I'll call you Sunday if I can borrow some money."

Mr. Cintron nodded to me.

"Willis isn't home," she said. "Just me. What time

are you going to call Sunday?"

"If I call at eight in the morning will that be too early?"

"No, I'll be up," Icy said. "And you'd better call. What did you want Willis for?"

"I wanted to know—I wanted to know if he's heard anything about Freddy," I said.

"Freddy Booker, that light-skinned boy that was in your case?"

"Yeah, just tell Willis—"

"He got arrested."

"Willis?"

"No, that Freddy. I don't know why he got arrested. Probably drugs, because that's what he does. He's pretty much messed up," Icy said. "You want me to ask around?"

"No!" I heard myself holler into the phone. "Look, Icy, don't say nothing to anybody. I'll call you Sunday, okay?"

"Eight o'clock."

It took me a minute to come down off the phone call and tell Mr. Cintron I didn't really know what Freddy was doing. "I know he got arrested but I don't know what he was doing."

"Why are you upset?" Mr. Cintron asked.

"That was my baby sister on the phone," I said. "I don't like her knowing who got arrested and who using drugs and everything. You know, she should just be going to school."

"If Freddy got arrested, he's probably looking to bring as many people into the case as he can," Mr. Cintron said.

"Why would he want to bring me into it?" I asked. "I didn't do anything to him. Even when our case went down, he was the one who turned me in. I didn't snitch him out."

"He sounds like a career thug," Mr. Cintron said. "And there are two good reasons to bring you into the case. If you did anything, or if he can pin something on you, he can cooperate with the prosecution and hope to get a lighter sentence. If you didn't do anything and went on trial with him and you looked innocent, then maybe the jury would let him slide because the overall case was weak. Remember what I told you about those crabs?"

"You think that shit is correct?" I asked.

"No, but I think it's the life you're in when you walk through some of the doors you've been walking through," he said. He stood up.

"You going to loan me the money to call Icy on Sunday?"

He looked at his calendar. "I'll be in Sunday morning for about an hour," he said. "You get your breakfast Sunday morning and I'll have Pugh or whoever's on let you eat it in here and make the phone call. Okay?"

"Yes."

"And try not to get into a fight with anybody between now and then."

CHAPTER 26

"So you got funded?"

"No, I did not get *funded,* Mr. Robinson," Miss Rossetti said. "I am just doing the job that I am scheduled to do."

"This is the second group meeting we've had this month," Play went on.

"And with your kind permission, sir, we will continue," Miss Rossetti said.

"Yes, ma'am." Play was wearing a half smile like he owned it and slouching in his chair with his legs stretched out in front of him.

There was a new girl in the group, and she was fine as she wanted to be. She looked a little Spanish, with dark hair and eyes, but I wasn't sure.

"In our last session we discussed what made us afraid," Miss Rossetti said, looking around the room. "This time I want to know what each of you feels you can do to make someone else happy. And we'll start with Mr. Robinson. I think your first name is . . . Eddie?"

"I let people I like call me Play."

"What shall I call you?" Miss Rossetti asked.

"That all depends on how attracted to me you are," Play said. "If you think me and you can be—"

"You can start, Mr. Robinson," Miss Rossetti said, her voice rising. "What do you think you could do to make someone else happy?"

"I could make my parents happy if I got a good job," Play said. "Maybe tighten up a gig with the post office. Nine to five. They would dig that big-time."

"That's a good observation," Miss Rossetti said. "You show very good understanding of what someone else feels and thinks. How about you, Deepak? You want to run with the ball?"

"My parents would be happy if I became an engineer," Toon said. "I wouldn't be as good an engineer as my brother, but that would make them happy, I think."

"Very good. Paola?" She was speaking to the new girl.

"My parents would be happy if I let my grandmother adopt my son," Paola said. "If she adopted him legally, then she could get ADC and she would be eligible for Section Eight housing on her own. Plus, she could get some start-up money from Family Services to help her set up her own place. And they even speak Spanish down there."

"You going to let her adopt your kid?" King Kong asked.

"Uh-uh." Paola shook her head. "I only got a five-year bid, and if God is on my side, I can walk in three, maybe even two and a half. Then if I can find somebody to hook up with, I can get my son back if he's in the foster system. But if the legal thing goes through with my grandmother, I can't get him back because my moms is going to want to keep Abuela on welfare so she don't have to support her."

"That's very technical, Paola," Miss Rossetti said.

"Baby, you got to know the technical stuff to survive in New York," Paola said. "The other thing I could do to make my parents happy is to marry some rich dude, but that ain't hardly happening because you got to be hooked up even to meet a rich dude."

"You never know what love will produce," Miss Rossetti said. "Mr. Right might just come along. You're a very attractive young woman."

"Honey, there's so many women out there ready to satisfy any man who comes along that pretty ain't hardly cutting it. Being smart isn't enough, and being nice isn't enough," Paola said. "I've got a baby and a jail record. Don't even talk to me about no Mr. Right."

Miss Rossetti took a deep breath and smiled. She didn't call King Kong's name but she kind of gestured toward his dumb butt.

"What I would like to do to make somebody else happy is to have my own place, you know." King Kong pulled at his crotch. "Right now—not right now but before I came up here—I was living in the shelter. Really, I was living in two shelters. Sometimes I stayed uptown with the folks, you know, on 126th Street. That was okay and I could deal with it. I was also spending some time downtown with the white folks because I thought that was interesting. I mean, downtown was where you had a whole different set of people—"

"But how would you make someone else happy, Mr. Sanders?"

"Well, you know, I'm thinking—if I had my own place, I could invite a girl up to the place and have some wine or something or maybe order out some fried chicken and have it up there or maybe even I could have my cousin drop by and check out my crib. Then he would see that I was doing okay and he could split and think maybe he would drop by again if he was in the neighborhood. He wouldn't be falling out behind that scene but maybe it would give him something else to do and that would make him happy."

"Very good," Miss Rossetti said. "What I particularly like is that none of your answers are egocentric. They all consider other people. How about you, Mr. Anderson?"

"I don't know," I said. "You know, you talking about what we would do and what we would say and whatnot, but if I said I would run around the park and jump up and dance and that would make my moms happy, what would you say? You would say that you can't do that because you locked up in here. If I said I would go over to Riverside Park and play two-on-two basketball against those white boys that come over to the park on weekends—they can play some ball—you would say that I can't do that because I'm in jail."

"That's right, but there are things—"

"Yo, let me run it, Miss Rossetti. Okay?"

"Go ahead."

"Okay, what I'm saying is that this isn't my world you're talking about. I can dig what you're saying about going with somebody else's feelings and what they're thinking instead of just dealing with what's on your mind. But I know there's a curtain that divides your world from mine."

"Because you're black, you mean?"

"You sure jumped on that in a heartbeat," Kat said.

"Kat, I'm trying to figure out where Mr. Anderson is going, that's all," Miss Rossetti said.

"It ain't just about black and white," I said. "I got this friend of mine who's white. So, he was in a war and he got captured. Nothing he could do except what they told him. Then the war was over and his family didn't do nothing for him. Then he got old and ended up in a nursing home."

"How old is your friend?" Miss Rossetti asked.

"About seventy-six, maybe seventy-seven," I said.

"He wasn't in no war because you can't be in a war if you that old," King Kong said.

"The guy he's talking about wasn't always that old," Leon said. "My grandfather was in a war back in the day when they was fighting the Vietnams. There's always a war going on."

"Mr. Anderson?"

"Yeah, well, him getting caught up in a war meant that he couldn't do what he thought was right," I said. "And then he came out the war and he wasn't getting on too tough, and then he got old and, like, feeble. At first he told me he was kicking it big-time, being a hero to his family and getting presents and visits and stuff all the time, but then, when the hammer fell, I found out that he was just scraping by."

"He was fronting and grunting," Kat said.

"Yeah, but that doesn't mean he didn't have his head together," I said. "I think he had his head together but it didn't make any difference. He couldn't make anybody else happy, and he couldn't make himself happy."

"Why did you become his friend?" Toon asked.

"That doesn't make any difference," I said.

"It makes a difference to me," Toon said.

"That's because you and Toon sweet on each other," King Kong said.

"Me and your mama sweet on each other, too," I said. "But the ASPCA don't like me messing with her."

"That's enough!" Miss Rossetti's voice rose to the ceiling.

Mr. Pugh had been sitting across from us playing solitaire on the computer, but soon as he heard Miss Rossetti's voice, he jumped up and started toward us. King Kong stood and took a step toward me but then turned and looked at Mr. Pugh and sat down again.

Yeah. Both of us knew he didn't want any more of me.

Miss Rossetti held her hand up to keep Mr. Pugh back and things got real quiet.

Mr. Pugh had about four different faces. He had his normal face which was like maybe he was lost. He had a smiling face, which was like maybe he was lost but he didn't care. He had his mad face, which looked like he wanted to kill you, and then he had this face that kind of darkened with his eyes darting around, like, "Hey, please give me a half of an excuse to turn your ass inside out." When he got that face on, I didn't even look at him, just down at the floor.

"Okay, so Mr. Anderson's friend was making up parts of his life," Miss Rossetti said as she sat back down. "Is that all bad?"

"If you got a police record it's not bad," Leon said. "Because the truth isn't going to help you in the real world."

"I don't recommend lying," Miss Rossetti started, "but I do understand your point. Mr. Anderson, can you think of anything that would make somebody else happy?"

"No, but I need to because I'm going to call my sister Sunday and I really would like to say something to her to make her happy. She hates me being in jail and I hate being here away from her. So I would like to think of something to say to her that would—but I can't tell her no lies."

"She's only nine, right?" Play asked.

"Yeah."

"Tell her you'll buy her a bracelet when you get

out," he said. "Girls like jewelry and she'll like it because you bought it for her."

"Is she smart?" Kat asked.

"She's my sister, ain't she?" I said.

"Yo, bro, we're not in Harvard," Kat said. "This is jail."

Everybody cracked on that.

"Yeah, she's real smart," I said.

"I agree with Little Ears," Paola said. "She can even imagine the bracelet or look for a nice one in the stores."

"Little Ears?" Play was touching his ears.

"Maybe you could write a book about her life," Toon said. "I think she would like that very much."

"Yeah, that's good thinking," I said. "She'd like that."

Toon smiled.

The group thing ended and we went straight to dinner. I was hungry as anything but they had cabbage, some kind of chopped-up ham, and scrambled eggs. I ate the cabbage and the eggs and left the ham. For dessert they had the same old, same old ice cream, but this time they had potato chips instead of pound cake. Lame for days.

"When I get out of here, all I'm going to eat for the next five years is steak," Play said.

"How come you didn't say nothing when that girl called you Little Ears?" I asked him.

Play just grinned. "I think she's trying to get with me. I hope she makes it."

Saturday morning I got a call from the precinct. Detective Rhodes asked me if I had made my mind up yet.

"About what?"

"Do the math," he said. "Twenty years or three. Which do you want?"

"I got to think about it," I said.

"You got to *think* about it?" He sounded surprised. "We'll pick you up Monday. You got forty-eight hours to decide where you're going to spend the rest of your life. You'd better think hard, my man."

The phone clicked off.

My stomach began to cramp and I just wanted to puke. When Mr. Pugh took our group to breakfast,

I joined the sick line. What I wished, what I really wished, was that I was getting the drugs that some of the kids at Progress got every day. Play told me that those drugs helped them get through the day. God knew I was needing something to get me through.

Saturday was forever long. Sadness was like sucking on me and taking the life out of my body. I felt so weak, I was having trouble standing up. There was no way I could make twenty calendars. I'd be thirty-five when I got out—if I got out. I'd probably meet some freak like King Kong or Cobo in jail and get killed. On the other hand, I didn't want to cop to a three bid, either. Any way I looked at the situation, it was foul.

My mind went back to the doctor's office. I didn't remember taking anything but the prescription pads. It was a storefront office with the entrance on Frederick Douglass Boulevard. There was one of those decals from a security service in the window plus a gate that came down over the door. In the alley, which you could get through from a building on 147th Street, there was a back door that just had one lock on it. There was a decal on that, too. Earlier I had gone past the place with Freddy and sat outside while he went in. When Freddy came out, he showed me the prescription pad with the numbers printed on it.

"That's his official New York State number," he said. "He put the pad back in his upper right-hand drawer."

That night I took a jimmy bar to the alley, found the door, and waited for a while until I was pretty sure that everything was clear. The doctor wasn't American and didn't live in the nabe, so I knew he wouldn't be there.

Three minutes. That's what I had given myself to get in, find the pads, and get out. By the time the alarm went off and the police arrived and looked at the front door, it would be at least five or seven minutes, I figured. Then they might just split because they would think it was a false alarm. It would take them at least five minutes if they checked the back door, and I'd be in the wind.

I said a quick prayer before I went after the door. I popped the door real quick and I was in. Soon as I got the door closed, I looked around and saw that I was in the doctor's back room. I tried his desk and it was open. The first pads I looked at didn't have the numbers Freddy had shown me, but the next three did. I snatched them, put them in my pocket, and was thinking about looking for some more when I thought I heard something out front. I panicked and got up out of there. There had been a few bills on the desk, but I didn't even stop for them. I knew I didn't pick up any drugs and I knew that all I gave to Freddy were the prescription pads.

I was innocent, but it didn't matter if the police said I was guilty. Soon as the jury looked over and saw you sitting at the defendant's table, they figured you must have done something.

CHAPTER 28

Sunday. Mr. Cintron called and said he wasn't coming in after all, but he told Mr. Wilson to let me take my breakfast into the administration office so I could use the phone.

"Hey, Icy, what's up?"

"I'm up, Willis is in bed, Mommy's in bed, and Sheba is up." Icy's speech was clear and precise. "Ask me who Sheba is."

"Okay, who's Sheba?"

"The woman who owns the bodega on the corner gave her to me," Icy said. "She's smoky gray with a small white spot on her chest. She doesn't say meow yet. She just kinda squeaks."

"A kitten. How old is she?"

"The woman said she's six weeks old but I took her to school and my teacher said she's closer to four weeks."

"You have to take good care of her," I said.

"I will. You want to know what I found out about Freddy?"

"Didn't I tell you . . ." The girl was getting me upset but I didn't want to yell at her. "Icy, didn't I tell you not to be checking out those thugs?"

"Okay, so I won't tell you what I found out," Icy said. "Even though it's kind of interesting."

"You know if I could get to you, I'd have to give you a punch in the nose, right?"

"So what do you plan to do today?" she asked.

"Probably play some ball, watch some television, check out the planes passing by," I said. "I like to watch the planes flying overhead and wondering where they're going. Other than that, I'm just killing time."

"You ought to catch a bird and raise it," Icy said. "I saw a movie—"

"The Birdman of Alcatraz," I said. "We saw that in here about two months ago and everybody was glad they weren't in no Alcatraz. If I do something long

term, it won't be raising birds for your cat to kill."

"It's beneath Sheba's dignity to kill birds," Icy said.

"If I get that much time on my hands, maybe I'll write a book about you."

"And we can get Spike Lee to do the movie," Icy said. "And I'll get a real cute baby to play me just born and then I'll play myself when I get older and I'll have Evan Ross play my boyfriend. Then when they have the Oscars, I'll wear an eggshell-white gown covered with white lace."

"Whoa . . . you got your acceptance speech all figured out yet?" I asked.

"No, but I will by next Sunday," she said. "Can you call me every Sunday?"

"I don't think so," I said. "But I'll try."

"You still don't want to hear about Freddy?"

"What about him?"

"Well, his cousin's best friend is in my best friend's class, and she told her that Freddy got arrested because he sold some dope to a white girl—a rich white girl—and she died."

"Get out of here!"

"They arrested Freddy, his half-brother, his uncle,

and some West Indian guy who was just over at their house having lunch," Icy said. "His cousin's best friend said that they can't prove it, but they're arresting everybody they can until they get the right evidence."

"Yeah, yeah, that's interesting. Okay, but don't be asking anybody any more questions," I said. "Can you make me a promise not to do that?"

"Okay."

"Yo, Icy, don't have me sitting up here in this place worried about you, okay?"

"Okay, I won't," she said. "You want to say hello to Sheba?"

"She near the phone?"

There was a moment of silence and then Icy said, "Now."

"Hello, Sheba."

"She heard you," Icy said. "You have to put her into the book. I don't know if I'm taking her to the Oscars, but you can put her in someplace. I don't really know if I want to go into acting first or college first. I probably won't be able to go to college."

"Why not?" I asked.

"I don't know," Icy said. "Not a lot of people from our block go to college."

"You're going," I said. "I'll pay for it."

"You will?"

"What school you want to go to?"

Mr. Wilson looked in and motioned for me to cut the phone.

"Look, I'm going to try to call you next Sunday," I said. "You take care of yourself and remember that promise you made me."

"I love you, Reese," Icy said.

"I love you, too, Icy," I answered. "I love you, too."

"Princeton."

"What?"

"Princeton is the school I want to go to," Icy said.

"You got it," I said. "Princeton."

CHAPTER 29

Mr. Wilson was getting on everybody's case on Monday during inspection. He was making sure all the beds were tight, and if they weren't he just yanked them out and threw the bedding on the floor.

"Whose room is this?"

"That's my room," Play said.

"What's this?"

"My toothbrush broke," Play said. "No shit, it just broke, man."

"I'm writing you up," Mr. Wilson said.

"You can beat that," Leon said. "Unless it got file marks on it."

Play would have a hearing, but there was no way he was going to beat it. If your toothbrush broke, you were supposed to turn it in for a new one right away. Or else they would say you were trying to make a shank.

I didn't know when the detectives from the city were going to come, but I was glad when Mr. Wilson turned me over to Mr. Pugh to go to Evergreen.

Being cuffed in the back of the van was foul, but I felt free at Evergreen. The staff treated me good and I had thought about working in someplace like Evergreen, taking care of senior citizens. Mr. Hooft had talked to me about me being a baker. That was good too. I didn't know anything about baking, but I thought I wouldn't mind giving it a try.

Mr. Pugh had taken me into the lobby and was about to go when the receptionist called him back. She handed him an envelope.

"This is Mr. Anderson's paycheck," she said, looking from me to Mr. Pugh. "We don't know how you handle it."

"He gets paid?" Mr. Pugh asked.

"I get paid?" I asked.

"If you work here, you get paid," the receptionist said. "We get paid once a month."

"Okay, I'll take it to the facility," Mr. Pugh said.

"See how much it is," I said.

"You probably won't get any of this," Mr. Pugh said, shoving the envelope into his jacket pocket. "You owe society—we don't owe you."

I was smiling when I went upstairs. I hadn't even thought of myself as having a job or making money, but I guess I was. When I got to my floor, Simi was pushing a pail of water across the floor. It was a large aluminum pail and had wheels on it.

"You want me to take that?" I asked.

"Oh, you're so big and strong!" she said. She felt the muscle in my arm and rolled her eyes.

A woman down the hall had died, and Simi had to clean out and disinfect the room. She said that was the policy. She said Mr. Hooft could wait if I wanted to help her.

We scrubbed every bit of the room with a brush and disinfectant, which she poured into the hot water. It stunk something terrible, and once or twice I thought I was going to throw up. We scrubbed and washed until eleven o'clock and then opened all the windows to let the room air out.

When I got to Mr. Hooft's room, he was mad.

"So you come anytime you want to now?" he

said, looking away from me.

"You missed me, man?" I asked him. "I was helping Simi clean the room down the hall."

"If the Japanese had captured you, they would have killed you right away," he said. "They called us all criminals, but with you, they would have been right!"

"You know what I was wondering?" I sat in the corner chair. "I saw some pictures of people in a German prison camp and they were skinny as anything. What did you get to eat?"

He looked over at me for a second, then away. Then he must have remembered something, because he gave a little jump and started laughing.

"You know what rijsttafel is?" he asked.

"No."

"It's a big bowl of rice with lots of side dishes. You can have curried meats, or vegetables, sweet or not sweet, soups, whatever you want," Mr. Hooft said. "But when the Japanese had us, they gave us strontstafel, little brown balls of rice mixed with cabbage. It was awful. We were always hungry, but no one died of hunger among the children or the women. Some of the men died from being worked so hard, and some died from the beatings or if they got sick. Some just gave up."

"It must have been rough," I said.

"Life is rough," Mr. Hooft said. "You didn't know that?"

"I thought you had it easy after you got out, the way you were talking and everything, but you just made some of that up, right?"

"Everything in life is made up," Mr. Hooft said. "You make up that you are happy. You make up that you are sad. You make up that you are in love. If you don't make up your own life, who's going to make it up for you? It's bad enough when you die and everybody can make up their own stories about you."

The doctor came in with Nancy Opara. He asked Mr. Hooft how he was doing.

"Why, do you need somebody to practice medicine on?" Mr. Hooft asked. "Maybe you have an extra needle you need to stick somewhere."

"Don't be so mean, old man!" Nancy said. "The doctor just has to check you out."

"I would rather be mean than be an African!" Mr. Hooft said.

"Yes, darling." Nancy started to close the door,

then pointed at me and motioned for me to leave.

"Come back later, Reese, and help me count my fingers and toes so these thieves can't get them," Mr. Hooft said. "You're the only one I can trust in here."

"Yes, sir."

Simi was in the hallway and asked if I wanted to go to the cafeteria. I said yes, and we went up and she bought two orange sodas. She'd started to tell me about her grandson when her pager went off.

"My husband. I know what he wants. He works in a restaurant in New Rochelle and he's going to try to convince me that whatever they're having there on special he should bring home for us to eat tonight. What a cheap man. I'm going to go get my cell phone and call him."

Simi left, and I watched as two women in wheelchairs came off the elevator and rolled up to the counter.

Sitting alone in the cafeteria, watching some of the residents getting their lunch on the far side of the room, I felt a sadness come over me. It was like a window had opened and a bad wind was pouring in from the outside. This was what I wanted, to be alone and not having someone watching me or locking a door behind me or cuffing me to a wall. I didn't want to have to fight anyone or watch my back every minute of the day. But that wasn't what my life had become. I wanted to be alone, but everyone I came into contact with had something over me, able to put me in detention or in juvy for more years.

My mind went back to the call from the detectives. I wondered if they were going to come pick me up this evening. I imagined them in their car driving along the highway, talking about what they did over the weekend, listening to the news. I knew I hadn't done what they were saying, but it really didn't matter. Some girl had died and they were making sure that somebody was going to pay for her death.

On the street, before I got arrested, I was Maurice Anderson. I wasn't living no big-time life, but I was me. Now I wasn't me but what I had done. The rules were different for a felon.

Three years or twenty years, the detective had said. What kind of choice was that? Just thinking about twenty years was like dying. Mr. Pugh had once said that I should get down on my knees and thank God I was in a juvenile facility.

"This is paradise," he had said.

It wasn't no paradise. There were rolls of barbed wire along the fences, doors that slammed shut behind you, and doors that were locked in front of you. And guards. I imagined them going home every day to their families. Maybe they talked about Progress. Maybe they just showered and tried to get the stink of us off their bodies. I don't know.

Twenty years had to be dying, had to be hell. Being in a prison with grown men, with gangs, and knowing that the whole world thought you were garbage.

Three years was the good thing they were offering. All I had to do was say yes and move my head away from going home. Just stop looking out the window wishing I could take a walk without thinking about where I was going and start thinking about how I was going to manage to keep myself in one piece for three more years.

Crying wanted to come. In a way it was like Reese was dead and it was me, whoever I was, whatever I was, grieving over him. Maybe I should get a tattoo, R.I.P. on my chest, so whenever I looked in the mirror I could see it.

I started thinking about my case again. When I

first got arrested, I thought maybe I would walk. Then I saw the list of charges and I thought it was a joke. Nobody was laughing. If Freddy and his people all testified that I gave him drugs, I was dead meat.

And what I didn't want to think about, the thing that was like chewing on my insides, was what I would do if I did get out. They'd probably put me in some wack school where you didn't learn nothing and just sat in class all day wondering where you were going to get some pocket money. They said that most of the people from 'round my way who go to jail once, go back again. Maybe even when they were out, there wasn't nothing there for them but a road back.

"Everything in life is made up," Mr. Hooft had said.

I wanted to make up a life. I could imagine myself walking down the street holding my head up high like I wasn't concerned about anything. I tried dreaming up a nine-to-five deal making maybe six or seven hundred bucks a week. But every time I started imagining what I might be doing, the detective's voice kept coming through.

"We'll be up there Monday to bring you back to the city," he had said.

I thought I could get up and just walk down the stairs and out into the street. What would happen? Someone would miss me and the police would start looking for me. Where would I go? What would I do?

Tired. Tired and sad. It was better to get mad at somebody and fight than just to feel so tired and sad all the time. The idea came to me, came like I should have known it all the time, that tired and sad was how I always felt. I knew I had to get to someplace else, someplace where I wasn't tired and I wasn't beat down and sad.

Miss Rossetti and people like her didn't seem sad, but they didn't have my life, not knowing what was going down next or what was going to be shaking when you went home, or the mirrors where you look in them and don't see nothing you like.

I could walk out and let the cops come and get me. Maybe I would pull my hand out my pocket real fast and they would think I had a gun. Maybe that would be better than twenty years. Or maybe the same.

CHAPTER 30

Icy didn't deal with stuff the way I did. She was all about what was going to go down and wasn't tied down to what had already happened. That's what I would have liked to have. Put Progress out of my head forever and move on like nothing had happened. No break-in, no getting arrested, no sitting in the courtroom listening to people talk about how much of my life they were going to take away, no crying in the van up to the facility.

Before I got to Progress, I didn't know time had a weight to it. My sentence was already too heavy to carry around all the time and I was praying for a release date. I couldn't wrap my head around getting out from under three more years. That was just too much of a load.

I thought about detention. I had dealt with it even though some dudes cracked up from being by themselves all the time. Maybe I could learn to deal with three more years. Then, when I got out, I'd move to another city. Maybe in the South, because I had never been there. I'd do any kind of work, sweep floors or mop and live in a small room, and I'd send any money I'd make to Icy so she could go to college. In three years, Icy would be twelve. I'd work until she was eighteen to help pay for her education. Then, if I kicked off, she could make up good stories about me.

I hated the idea of three more years, because it was already making my stomach turn. I didn't see what else I could do. I couldn't take a chance on a twenty bid.

"Where are you, Reese?" Simi's voice startled me. "Boy, you looked like you were a million miles away!"

"Just thinking," I said.

"You come up with something good?" she asked, hands on her hips.

"I don't know," I said.

"Life goes on, honey," she said. "Sometimes it seems hard, but you have your whole life ahead of you. Don't forget that. Now come on downstairs with me, because the woman in three eighteen is complaining that I didn't sweep her floor and is threatening to write to the president."

CHAPTER 31

We cleaned 318 with the woman standing in the doorway complaining the whole time. Then I went back to Mr. Hooft's room and he told me how mean the doctor had been to him.

"All doctors like to hurt people," he whispered to me. "They just pretend to help you!"

"That's not true," I said. "They don't want to hurt people."

"Come over here," he said. "Sit next to me."

I was surprised, but I sat on the bed next to him. He put his hand on mine. "You should always try to be a good boy," he said. "It's better that way. Then you won't be in jail. You going to try?"

"I'll try," I said.

He motioned for me to go away and I went and

sat in the chair. I felt a little funny, but really glad because I knew he was trying to be my friend. Like Toon was trying, and it was hard for all of them. And for me.

Mr. Pugh was talking to Father Santora in the lobby when I went down at four.

"Everybody likes Reese," the priest was saying. "He's a fine young man and a good worker."

"Okay, so maybe I won't shoot him on the way back to the facility," Mr. Pugh said.

Father Santora laughed and the receptionist laughed, but I didn't think it was all that funny.

Mr. Pugh sat me up in the front of the van and cuffed me to the grating that separated the cab from the back.

"You think I might overpower you and escape?" I asked.

"I used to play right tackle for Mississippi," he said. "I could crush your black ass with one hand and eat a sandwich with the other hand."

He acted kind of pissed off and I didn't say anything else. I was glad to sit in front instead of bouncing around in the rear. We drove through the city and I could see dudes just strolling and taking care of their business and it reminded me again of how much I wanted to be free.

"You like Spanish girls?" Mr. Pugh asked me as we passed a crowd of kids.

"I like all girls," I said.

"I never hear you guys talking about girls," he said. "If I was locked up, I'd be thinking about girls all the time."

"If you were locked up, you'd be thinking about getting free all the time," I said. "You can't be in jail and think like you're out in the world."

"So I hear you're in trouble again," he said.

"They're talking about some charge I don't know anything about," I said. "They said I stole some drugs from the doctor's office two years ago and gave them to the guy who was arrested the same time I was. He messed with the drugs and somebody died or something, and they want to run a homicide charge on me."

"You do what they said?"

"No, but it don't matter," I said. "When I was on trial before, I looked over at the jury and they looked at me, and I could tell they were going to toast me. I go to trial again, the same thing is going to happen. The detectives said that they might give me a chance to cop to a lesser and pull a three instead of a twenty."

"Oh, yeah?" Mr. Pugh looked at me. "That's a good break for you, huh?"

"I don't know, I guess."

"What you going to plead guilty to?"

"I don't know," I said. "They didn't tell me yet."

Some brothers walked in front of the van and stopped in the middle of the street. One was on his cell phone. Mr. Pugh hit his horn and one of the brothers grabbed his crotch with one hand and gave Mr. Pugh the finger with the other.

Mr. Pugh hit his horn again and the brother came over to the driver's side. Mr. Pugh pulled his gun and held it on his lap.

"Yo, bitch!" The black guy reached in and grabbed Mr. Pugh by the collar.

Mr. Pugh grabbed the guy's wrist and put the gun right under his chin. "Is your mama in heaven, boy?" he asked. "And do you want to go see her? Is that why you need to mess with a cop this afternoon?"

"Hey, I'm just playing, officer."

Two of the other dudes came over and started cursing but backed off when they saw Mr. Pugh's gun.

"Now, I got to get the criminal with me back to

jail," Mr. Pugh said. "But I got room in the back if you need a lift."

"No, man, I'm good," the brother said.

Mr. Pugh let him go and the guy backed away. Mr. Pugh put the gun back in his holster as we moved off.

"You know how much I love that?" he asked.

"Yeah, I got an idea," I said.

We drove for ten more minutes before he said anything else, but he kept looking at me like he wanted to say something. I hoped he wasn't going off or something. When he did speak, I didn't know what he was talking about.

"You know what my daddy used to say?" he asked. "He used to say that the snake that's gonna kill you is probably wearing your damned shirt."

I waited for him to say something else, but he didn't.

We didn't talk anymore until we got to Progress and he was uncuffing me.

"Why did you say a snake was going to be wearing your shirt?" I asked him.

"I didn't say it," Mr. Pugh said. "That was what my daddy used to say. He meant that if somebody was going to mess you up, it was probably going to be you."

I thought back to what we had been talking about before the brother came over to the car. Mr. Pugh had asked me what I was going to plead guilty to and I said I didn't know. I wondered if he was saying I shouldn't plead guilty to nothing. When he was patting me down, I wanted to ask him, but he finished real quick and was walking away before I got my thoughts together.

I was scared that the two detectives from Harlem would be waiting for me, but I didn't see them when I hit the corridor. Everybody was lining up for dinner and it was Play, instead of one of the regular guards, taking us into the dining room. Me and him sat together after we got our food, and I asked him if he had seen the detectives that afternoon.

"Yeah, they were looking for you, man," he said. "One of them had a ball and chain to tie around your ankle and the other one had one of those black-and-white-striped prison suits for you to wear."

"That's supposed to be funny, huh?"

"They know where you are," Play said. "If they wanted to come and get you, they wouldn't be riding all the way up here. They probably would have had Mr. Pugh just drop you off at Alcatraz or wherever."

"Alcatraz is in California," I said.

"Then they could fly you in one of those prison planes," Play said. "Remember that picture with Nicolas Cage?"

"Yeah."

I told him I remembered the picture, but that didn't stop Play from telling me the whole story again.

While Play talked, I was wondering about what Mr. Pugh had said and what he meant. I didn't want to catch a twenty bid, but I knew I couldn't tell what was going to happen if I went on trial.

The food didn't go down and I asked the cook for two apples when I turned my tray in.

"No," he said.

"I can't eat now," I said. "My stomach is upset."

"No."

I would have loved to punch him right in his greasy face.

What I told myself was that the detectives wouldn't come after six, but I kept looking at the door anyway. Every time it opened, my heart jumped a little.

The word was out that Toon got a release date.

"Yo, Toon, what's the first thing you're going to do when you get home?" I asked him. Me and Play had sat with him off to the side of the rec room.

"Maybe I'll try to memorize one book in school," Toon said, pushing his glasses up on his nose. "I think if I memorize one whole book then I can just work on the other ones and get better grades."

"Hey, I might try that too," Play said.

"You going back to school?" I asked.

"I got to unless I go into one of those special programs they have in the Bronx," Play said. "I got to get either my GED or diploma if I want to go to college one day."

"I would like to get into a good high school," Toon said.

"You will," I said. "You're smart enough."

"Brothers always says that," Toon said. He looked down but I saw he was smiling.

Eight thirty was lights-out, but I didn't mind. I was tired anyway.

When I woke up, it was three seventeen in the morning. There was some scuffling in the hallway and I kept real still to hear what was going on, but I couldn't tell. I thought I heard Mr. Wilson's voice. Then everything was quiet.

I remembered the dream I had been having. Icy was a movie star and I was a photographer taking her picture. She was walking on that red carpet in front of a light blue board—maybe sky blue—and she was with Paris Hilton, Mariah Carey, and Alicia Keys. Then Bow Wow got into the dream and he was escorting her and all the while I was snapping pictures like a professional. Every once in a while she would look over at me and give me a big smile and I was snapping perfect pictures and she was looking better than all the other women there. It was a boss dream.

Six thirty formation. Mr. Cintron had us.

"You guys have problems, you need to come to a staff member and talk about it," he said. "I realize that's not always easy, but you need to give it a try. Last night we had to transfer Trevedi to the L wing. I hope we don't have to transfer anybody else. Anderson, you see me after breakfast."

I didn't know why they had to transfer Toon to the L wing, but it usually meant that he had went off or something.

At breakfast, Leon said that Toon had tried to hang himself.

"Didn't he get a date?" Play asked me.

"Yeah." I remembered Toon in the visiting room with his parents yelling at him and then him saying how he was never as good as his brother. Toon knew about home.

Mr. Cintron didn't look too anxious when he told me to see him after breakfast, and when I went to his office, his secretary didn't say anything, so I thought it wasn't about the detectives. I sat there for five minutes on the wooden bench before he called her and told her to send me in.

"Okay, Reese, so you've got seventy-two dollars in your account now," he said. "You made minimum wage, which added up to a hundred thirty-four dollars, but they took out taxes, and we're charging you for transportation to and from the senior citizens' home."

"You're charging me for Mr. Pugh driving me back and forth?" I asked.

"Yeah, and you're lucky, because we're only charging you per mile and not for his time, or you wouldn't be getting anything," he said. "You can use the money to make phone calls and to spend four dollars a week at the commissary. Do you understand that?"

"Yeah."

"If you abuse the money in any way, I'll just take it all as a fine, do you understand that?"

"Yeah."

"That's it," he said. "Go to your first class."

"How's Toon?" I asked.

"Toon?"

"Trevedi."

"He'll live," Mr. Cintron said. "He's a little depressed, but he'll get over it."

"Can I ask another question?"

"About Trevedi?"

"About those detectives," I said. "They said on the

phone they were coming up yesterday."

"They've dropped it," Mr. Cintron said.

"Just like that?" My voice went way up and I felt weak all over. My brain went black—nothing was in it for a few seconds. I wanted to cry and not cry at the same time. "Just like that? They just *dropped* it?"

"You were pretty worried, weren't you?"

"They were talking about three years or twenty years and I didn't know—I didn't know what to do," I said. "Sometimes I was thinking about pleading not guilty because I didn't do anything, but I didn't want to risk no twenty bid."

"Sit down, Anderson," Mr. Cintron said. "Look, if you run across the street in the middle of the day dodging traffic, you might get hit by a truck or a bus and get seriously hurt or killed; but if you make it to the other side, you're home free, out of danger. But if you commit a crime, a felony . . . you pick up a gun or a knife and do some serious harm or commit an aggravated felony, you put yourself at risk for the rest of your life. Anytime something happens near you, they're going to be looking in your direction to see if you had anything to do with it.

"And if you hang with people who put themselves

at risk, you're going the same route. It's like running with a pack of starving dogs. The only thing you're going to know about them is that if they think you're weak, they'll eat you in a heartbeat."

"But those two detectives . . ." I looked around the room. My feeling of relief was turning to being mad. "They were acting like they had a done deal. I think they were ready to burn me, man."

"They're human too," Mr. Cintron said. "And if they thought they were right, well, yeah, you're going to feel the heat. And this guy you were involved with—"

"Freddy."

"He doesn't care anything about you," Mr. Cintron said. "He'd put you in jail for twenty years to get a week off his time. That's the way these guys operate. You got to remember that this is the world you walked into when you opened the door back then."

"Yeah."

"I'll let you know how Trevedi is," Mr. Cintron said, standing. "Maybe you can even go talk to him. It might do him some good."

CHAPTER 33

"So I'm going to be having my hearing this afternoon," I said. Mr. Cintron had given me permission to visit Toon, and I was sitting on the chair at the end of his bed. "If everything works out, I'll be getting my date."

"I hope it works out for you," Toon said.

"Where does your family live?"

"In Brooklyn," Toon answered. "Do you know where Clinton Avenue is?"

"I don't know anything about Brooklyn," I said. "But I was thinking, maybe when we get out, we can hook up and hang out sometimes. That cool with you?"

"That's very cool with me."

"One of the problems of going back into the world is that it's the same world you were dealing with when you got into trouble," I said. "So it's going to be just as hard to deal with as it was then, but if you round up some homeboys on your side, it'll be easier."

"Or a brother," Toon said.

"Or a brother," I said, standing. "And I can't have my brother hurting himself. You know what I mean?"

Toon put his head down and his hands in his lap. I sat on the bed next to him and put my arm around him for a minute.

I was worried that Toon wasn't going to be all right. I thought he was going to go home with his parents and have them yell at him and go on about how he wasn't as good as his brother. That was crap.

"Be strong, man," I said as I left Toon's room. Mr. Wilson locked the door behind me, and I turned away from the window because I didn't want to see Toon sitting on his bed alone.

I was pretty sure my hearing was locked. Mr. Cintron told me he would be on the panel, and I knew he was in my corner. All I needed was to keep my mind correct and focused on what I needed to let them know.

Mr. Pugh was with me and talking stupid stuff about how it had been when he was a kid. I couldn't even imagine a bigheaded, bald dude like him being a kid.

"We didn't have none of the stuff you kids got now," he said. "We didn't have cell phones, iPods, nothing like that. My big brother got a computer in 1982. It had sixty-four K memory. I got a goldfish with more memory than that now."

"I didn't know you had a brother," I said. "What's he doing now?"

"Nothing." Mr. Pugh gave me his "shut up" look and I shut up.

The clock on the administration office wall said twenty past one when the two people on the panel and Mr. Cintron came back from lunch. I had been sitting in the office from five minutes to one and was getting a little nervous. They walked by me and it was a quarter to two before they called me in.

They had turned the table so that the long side was facing the door, and I sat in the middle across from Mr. Cintron, an older black dude with silver-white hair, and a really thin white woman who kept messing with the papers in front of her.

Mr. Pugh had come in with me and he sat in the corner.

"Maurice, as you know, I'm Frank Cintron," Mr. Cintron said. "This is Miss Carla Evans and Mr. Alan Shaw."

"How do you do?" I said.

They both nodded.

"Panel, this is Maurice Anderson," Mr. Cintron said, looking at me. "He was arrested for stealing prescription pads from a neighborhood physician and selling the pads to a known drug dealer. He pled guilty and was sentenced to a total of thirty-eight months which, under the good time standard, makes him eligible for release after thirty months, two weeks—"

"That would be eighty percent of his sentence?" the black guy asked.

"Yes. He's served twenty-six months, twenty-two at Progress, and his petition today is for an early release, which would reduce his effective time served by four months."

"Mr. Anderson, can you tell us in your own words why you deserve to be rewarded with an early release?" the white woman asked.

"I don't intend to get into any more trouble," I said. "I made a mistake but I've learned my lesson and I plan to do the right thing and avoid the kinds of people I was dealing with before."

"What lesson did you learn?" the black guy asked.

"Crime doesn't pay," I said.

"If it did pay, would you commit more crimes?"

"No, ma'am."

"So what are you going to be doing that's different than what you were supposed to be doing before you came to Progress?" Miss Evans asked.

"Work hard in school and maybe get a part-time job after school," I said.

"Why didn't you do that before?" the black guy asked.

"I didn't know I was supposed to have a strategy to deal with my situation," I said. "I was just, like, drifting from day to day. Now I know I need a plan to take care of business."

"And what's your plan?" the woman asked.

"Just keep to myself," I said. I felt like I was floating and she was looking at me funny.

"So you're promising to do better, but isn't the truth of the matter that you want to get out and so naturally you would make the kinds of promises that would get you out?" the woman asked. "What would be the difference if we were here the day after you were arrested? Wouldn't you have promised not to do it again if we let you go?"

"Yeah."

"What have you learned here at Progress that might help you turn your life around?" Mr. Cintron asked.

Mr. Cintron was opening the door for me and I was going blank. I looked at him and couldn't think straight, but I knew I had to say something.

"You know, everybody's got to survive," I said. "And if you don't think about how you're going to make it, then you just go with whatever is around you. I know I have to invent something, look around and figure out some way to survive that's not going to get me killed or get me back in the jail system. I think I can find something, because in my heart I know what I want and what I don't want. I don't want to spend the rest of my life being locked up or ducking and hiding."

"And you didn't know that before you started stealing—what was it?" The black guy started going through the file.

"Prescription pads," I said.

"You didn't know that then?"

"I knew I didn't want to be locked up," I said. "I knew that part of it, but what I didn't know was that you needed a strategy for your life. In here, I see people working their shows and trying to get over the best way they can. One guy I work with at Evergreen—"

"Maurice is part of our work program," Mr. Cintron said.

"He was a prisoner in a Japanese war camp and he was telling me how he survived," I said. "How he figured out how to live through the war and stuff. You know, some people didn't make it, and—"

"What is your plan to 'make it'?" the black man asked.

"I don't have a big plan," I said. "I'm fifteen and I got to go to school, but I'll do my best in school and I'll just live at home and do what I can to stay out of trouble. I know that I might not become great or anything like that, but if something bad does happen to me, I don't want to be the one to make it happen."

"Are you sorry for the crime you committed?"

"Yes, ma'am."

"Because you made yourself part of the problem in your community," she said. "Didn't you?"

"Yes, ma'am."

"And what's different now, Mr. Anderson?" she asked.

"What I want to do is to help my little sister go to college," I said. "I think if I keep my mind on that, just focus in on it, I can keep myself straight."

"You were living at home with your parents?" the black guy asked.

"Fairly dysfunctional situation," Mr. Cintron said. "Mother has a history of drug abuse."

"You saw that abuse at home and you still got involved with illegal drugs?" the black guy asked.

"Yes, sir."

"Has anyone in your family been to college?" Mr. Cintron asked.

"No, sir, that's one of the reasons I want to help Icy go to college."

"Icy?" The black guy took off his glasses. "Your sister's name is Icy?"

"It's really Isis, like the Egyptian goddess," I said. "But we call her Icy."

I was told to wait outside, and Mr. Pugh went with me.

"You did real good," he said. "You don't look that

smart, but you had some good things to say. You see Mr. Cintron nodding his head? He's going to vote for you."

"I hope so."

I wasn't sure. I had come up with some answers, but they didn't seem all that good to me. It was like they were asking me stuff that only had one right answer, and then when I gave them that right answer they were saying it was the same old stuff. I wanted them to know that I knew it was the same old stuff too. I was going back to the same old block, the same old family, the same old neighborhood. Everybody on the block who was messing with drugs or selling drugs had seen what I had seen. And a lot of them were going to be getting abused, too.

I had told them about Mr. Hooft's being in the children's camp and figuring out a way to survive by thinking about that flower. I wanted to tell them more about how Mr. Hooft and a lot of people really have to struggle just to make it from day to day. And even though we can lay out all the right answers, it doesn't always help. Maybe I should have told them about Icy's ideas, about dreaming up your future and then trying to make it happen.

The buzzer went off and the secretary motioned for me and Mr. Pugh to go back in.

Mr. Pugh took his place in the corner and I sat down in front of the desk.

"Mr. Anderson, it's the view of this panel that although you have shown some insight into your problems, you have also shown some behavior which indicates a lack of control," the woman said. "You've had several fights despite the special attention you've been given and the privilege of participating in the work program.

"We hope over the next four months you continue gaining a knowledge of what you have to do once you're released and bring that knowledge to bear in avoiding future involvement with the justice system," she went on. "We think your attitude and behavior are headed in the right direction, but at this time they are not worthy of being rewarded.

"I think it's commendable that Mr. Cintron has cast a dissenting vote," she said. "It shows that in his eyes, you have made considerable improvement. But, as the record clearly shows, you still have problems. Do you have anything you would like to put on the record at this time?"

"No, ma'am."

CHAPTER 34

"I know this is a disappointment." Mr. Cintron had called me from the rec room. "But it's only four months."

"No, sir, it's not just four months. It's what my life is about," I said. "People looking at me and hanging my record around my neck. That record is worse than those orange jumpsuits we wear. But it's okay in a way, because I need some time to figure out where I'm going to be starting from, you know what I mean?"

"Not exactly."

"Home might not be where it's at," I said. "And everybody is telling me the streets ain't where it's at. So I know I got to start with me, but even though I think I know me best—better than that black dude and that woman running her mouth—I don't know exactly where I'm at. If I was older and could catch a job, I would feel better about my chances, but I'm not older, so ain't no use in going there."

"You sound really discouraged," Mr. Cintron said.

"Yeah, but it's not just about the four months," I said. "It's more because my life is definitely on the raggedy side and everything down the road is looking hard."

"Reese, you know more than you did when you came in here," Mr. Cintron said. "You need to use that knowledge to keep yourself away from places like this. I think you're stronger than when I first met you too. You worked out all right at Evergreen because you controlled yourself and used your intelligence. You keep doing that and you can make it. Don't give up on yourself."

"I won't, sir. When I was in detention, I didn't have no choice but to keep to myself. I didn't have anybody on my case so I didn't have to throw down, and that was good. I just need to stay away from people who gave up on themselves. I know I'm going to run into some bad stuff, the same way Toon knows what he's facing. But I'm harder than Toon. I can look at that bad stuff and use it to remind me of what I don't need in my life.

"And what I said about Icy going to college? I meant that. I'm going to work on keeping myself correct so I can take care of her. I think I can handle this shit. I really do."

"See you in the morning." Mr. Cintron put his hand out. We shook hands and he stood like it was time for me to leave his office, which I did. I closed the door behind me and I guess he went on dealing with the things in his life, and I started dealing with the things in mine.

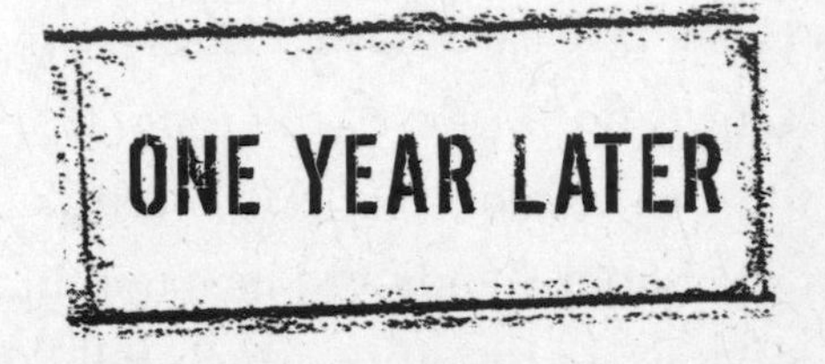

I've been out of Progress for almost one year now, and it's harder than I thought it was going to be. It took a lot to get to the point where I felt good about myself even once in a while. When I first got out, I told myself that I had to think hard before I did anything, no matter how tempting it was or how much it looked like a get over. That didn't work out too tough, not by itself, because even though it was the answer I knew I was supposed to come up with, it didn't help when I looked around and didn't see anything that made me feel different than all the other brothers I saw hanging out on the stoops or getting high in the park.

The thing was that the streets had their own

sense, a different view of what real was all about. I saw people living in that street world and all the time knowing how dangerous it was, how they could slip and fall through a hundred cracks that would leave them either dead or in some lockdown. I knew what was happening on the streets and how to deal with it, and even though I had an idea of what was going down in the outside world, I didn't know if I could ever really deal with it. But what I could do was keep my mind on Icy and college for her. It wasn't all I wanted in the world, but it was something to live for and I was cool with it.

I looked up Toon and he's not doing so good, but he's hanging in there too. I told him if he ever thought about hurting himself again he should call me and we could go out for a pizza or something.

"Pizza is better than dying," he said, looking down the way he always did.

Once we went to the park in Brooklyn and played two-on-two basketball and got killed by two Spanish dudes who went to Wadleigh. I was mad, but Toon thought it was the funniest thing that had happened and that lifted me up a little. Toon is all right. A little strange, but all right. I was glad to see him trying to keep himself together. Just looking at us you wouldn't think about us as being heroic or nothing, but I think sometimes we are.

Mom is still Mom. She's about the same, which is better than getting worse. She stumbles through her days, and it's almost like Icy is the woman of the house. Sometimes she makes me breakfast. Her eggs always stick to the pan, but I still eat them.

Willis is on Riker's Island. He says when he gets out he's going to make a rap CD. He knows in his heart that's not going to happen, but he's still running it.

I work after school at Evergreen, making minimum wage. By the time I buy stuff for school and buy food for me and Icy, the money's gone, but at least I'm not stealing.

Right after New Year's Day, Mr. Hooft died. He hadn't seemed that sick or anything, but one day he woke up and felt terrible. Simi said he seemed to know that he was going to die.

"Sometimes people know these things," she said.

He left a note with his silver soap dish. It read *Reese, keep this for me and do not get into any trouble. Your friend, Pieter.*

Mr. Cintron called once to see how I was. He said

that Play was at Bridges in the Bronx and headed for Highland upstate. He said that it made him sad to hear that. I believed him.

Sometimes at night, Icy comes into the living room where I sleep and sits on the end of the couch and we talk. She tells me about her plans and I tell her mine. I make stuff up for her and sometimes we pretend together. Icy believes in herself big-time, and you can see it when she talks about going to college and becoming a teacher or a lawyer. The longer I stay out of trouble, the more I'm beginning to believe in myself, too. It's like, okay, something good could happen.

I know in my heart that my life could still end up in the gutter or in jail. But, like Mr. Cintron said, I know more than I used to, and I'm stronger, too. I know what I got to do for Icy, and I know what I got to do for me, and I'll do it as long as I can and hope for the good parts.